The Vintage Vendetta

Secondhand Sleuth Mysteries
Book One

By
Mel Morgan

ISBN: 9798810618744

In memory of my own "Aunt Daphne,"
for inspiring my love of secondhand treasures.

1

WEDNESDAY

Drool was running down my face—I'd been dozing on the couch for at least an hour when I realized someone was knocking on my front door. No, not knocking—pounding. At least that's what it felt like inside my echoing skull as I pried my sticky self off the sofa and put a hand to my face.

There was a piece of cheddar stuck to my cheek where it had landed when I'd fallen asleep watching a movie the night before. The pajamas I wore would not look clean if I just brushed them off, so I gave up. Whoever was at my door was going to get me just as I was if they wanted me now, and the rhythmic pounding meant their need must be urgent.

My throat felt like sandpaper from sleeping with my mouth open, so I paused for a sip of water from one of the many half-empty bottles scattered around the room. It might be a mess, but at least they weren't wine bottles. Not yet, anyway.

When I got to the front door, I yanked it open, ready to end the incessant knocking. "What is so urgent this early in the morning?" I asked, trying not to sound as irritated or half-asleep as I was. I softened and started again when I saw the timid looking teenage kid on the other side flinch at my harsh greeting. By the look of the bright sun behind him cutting lasers into my retinas, it wasn't even early anymore.

"Yes? Can I help you?" I started again. He was wearing a bicycle delivery uniform, and he looked a little nervous about his job right now. I gave him a weak smile as an apology.

He didn't return it. "Are you Mrs. Jessica Weston?" the kid asked, after taking a step back from the door and straightening his shoulders to regain his composure. But he was wrong about my name.

"No, sorry, kid. I'm Miss J. Braun." I was about to head back in and close the door to end any further question of which name was mine. Whatever this kid was bringing, I didn't think it was going to be great news. It would be better for me if he took whatever doom he heralded back with him and marked it undeliverable.

Choosing this moment to become brave, he stuck his gangling leg out and wedged one long blue sneaker in the path of my door.

Touché, delivery kid.

I sighed. "OK, I was a Mrs. Weston in another life. Just trying to forget, sorry." I held my hand out, and he placed a thin white envelope into it before turning to flee in long bounds like a gazelle.

I closed the daylight out by shutting the door and turned to take in the war zone appearance of my apartment. Over the last couple of weeks, I had let it go. Empty takeout cartons and paperback mystery novels were strewn across every surface, and I hadn't opened the blinds in more days than I could remember. Wallowing in self-pity was a full-time job for me right now, since my last dead-end job had ended and my ex-husband, Charlie, had left for good.

I'd let myself go over that time period, too, apparently. Catching my reflection in the glass of the framed picture on the wall in the living room, I saw that there were bags under my large green eyes. The thirty-nine-year-old face that looked back at me was tired and a little sad. I saw the reflection of the thin white envelope in my hand. I remembered that whatever was in it was important enough to be sent by a private messenger instead of by routine mail delivery. But then again, I hadn't exactly been opening my mail lately, either. Or answering phone calls. After quitting my gig as a barista two weeks earlier, I had been hiding from the world.

Folding my legs underneath me, I sat on the hard leather couch that was a leftover from my life with Charlie. It was stiff and uncomfortable, and I'd never really liked it—kind of like our marriage. But the green monster had been what he wanted when we were shopping for furniture, and I had been happy to go along with whatever made Charlie shoot me his thousand-watt smile. Now I was stuck with the green leather boulder until I got it out of here and gained something else. But I didn't even know what else I wanted. I perched on one end awkwardly and returned my attention to my surprise delivery.

I slipped one thin finger under the edge of the flap and ripped the envelope open across the top, yanking out the folded paper inside. When it unfolded, it opened sideways, and I turned it around to see that it was a trifold card with an embossed cover printed in shades of gray and green.

An invitation? That's what it looked like, and sure enough, when I squinted at the overly curlicue script on the front, it read: *You Have Been Invited,* but it didn't look like any party or wedding invitation I had ever seen. There was nothing fun or inviting about it, and I wondered for a second if this was some strange new form of court summons, and if my ex-husband had some new proceedings he wanted to drag me through.

But the invitation wasn't from Charlie. I saw when I opened the first flap that flowers decorated the inside, though they were definitely not for a wedding. There were black roses delicately etched along leafy vines that wove around more fancy embossed writing: *Your presence is requested at the last audience and ceremony of remembrance for the late Ms. Daphne Marie Braun.* There was more, but I had stopped to reread that sentence twice more, my mouth again dry from hanging open.

Last audience and ceremony of remembrance? Was Aunt Daphne dead? Because that sounded like it had to be a funeral. Was I truly holding an invitation to the funeral of my beloved aunt, with no one calling to tell me about her passing?

Grief broke through the surprise, and I felt a lump start in my chest and tears form in my already reddened eyes. My sweet Aunt Daphne, who I had spent summers with as a child at my grandparents' house. My only aunt, who had always been there to listen to my teenage problems when my mother felt like an alien to me. She was gone. And I didn't even have the chance to say goodbye. That was the worst part—the regret of not having seen her since I moved out to Arizona with Charlie fifteen years earlier. I had been tired of Minnesota and thought that starting a new exciting life out West with a new exciting man would be just the thing to get

4

my life moving in the right direction. But now it felt like a wrong turn.

After fifteen years of being almost two thousand miles away from my family, all I had to show for it was some ugly furniture Charlie left behind, and a few thousand dollars in the bank. None of that could replace the time I had lost with my aunt. I missed her so much, and now it was too late.

I looked back down at the invitation in my hand and continued reading: *To be held at the family estate in Pine Grove, on Saturday, the fifteenth of May at midnight.* Midnight!? What kind of creepy funeral was that? Sure, Aunt Daphne had been a little eccentric. But planning her funeral for midnight seemed overly dramatic. And at the family estate, no less.

I thought back to the big log house in the small town of Pine Grove, Minnesota, where, as a kid, I had stayed every summer with my grandparents. It was like a mansion of mysteries to my Nancy Drew-addled ten-year-old mind. Set back in the tall pines, the house was a towering three stories of century-old architecture filled with plenty of odd rooms to explore. Aunt Daphne always lived there, having never left the nest, and as a child, I believed it was just because it was such a great place to be. Looking back on it as an adult, I thought she had probably stayed there because she was socially awkward and just never found the right way to start out on her own. I understood how someone could get stuck in a rut like that.

But what had happened to cause her death? If she had been ill, no one had told me that, either. But then again, who was there left to call me? Grandma and Grandpa Braun had been gone for many years now. And my mother, Daphne's sister, had been living "abroad," as she called it, for the last few years—which currently meant in a bus on a beach in Hawaii with a Buddhist monk half her age. That only left my mother's other sibling, Uncle Rick, who had always been in and out of trouble. He probably was still in Mistletoe County because I didn't think he'd ever have the means or ambition to go far from home. But he probably didn't know how to find me if his sister was dying. Or dead, which I was still holding the proof of in my hands.

Turning the dark invitation over, I noticed a handwritten message on the last fold, tucked down among the creepy dark roses. It was etched with blue ink in a stiff print, almost too small to read: *Ms. Weston, please contact me immediately regarding the property at 1701 Evergreen Circle.* Below the message was a signature, followed by a phone number. The name was indecipherable after the initials of D and E, and the words Legal Counsel, but the phone number was clear enough. I wasn't sure why a lawyer would contact me about my grandma's old house. Whatever the issue was, couldn't someone in Minnesota handle it?

Sitting on my green rock in my fuzzy pink pants and button-down pajama shirt was no way to confront a day that started off like this. I stood and stretched, feeling my recently added love handles roll a little. I walked down the short hallway to the bedroom I had shared with my ex-husband Charlie for so long and pulled on a light T-shirt and jeans. Stopping at the mirror over the dresser, I pulled my shoulder-length wavy brown hair up into a messy bun. Now I was comfortable and ready for coffee. No day was ever really started before I had some caffeine.

Walking into the small kitchen, I enjoyed the view out of the window above the sink, out onto the terrace behind the apartment building and beyond. The desert landscape of long horizontal sweeping lines of brown and red was still as beautiful to me as the first day I had driven to the Southwest and was impressed by its stark beauty. Just because my life here with Charlie had been a disappointment didn't mean I hadn't enjoyed the change of scenery.

Maybe today would be different. It had already started out differently. But first, caffeine. I brewed a strong cup of light roast, gave it a generous splash of heavy cream, and took a deep sip to center myself.

I went back into the living room and looked resentfully at the ugly couch that had caused my aching back and decided to remain standing. I needed to call the lawyer who had written the note on the invitation. I reached for my phone where it still sat on the coffee table after I tossed it, hands numb with sleep as I drifted off, and dialed the scribbled phone number.

As I paced around waiting for the call to connect, I noticed some mail on the side table under a box that read *Andy's Anchovy Palace: Best Pizza in Plainsborough*. The box was smeared with a grease stain that had soaked through the cardboard sometime last weekend.

Just as I thought I should head out to the mailbox to gather the rest of my mail, a recorded message picked up, to announce that I had reached the legal firm of Edwards, Gray, and Benson. "Hi, this is Jessica Br—Weston," I corrected myself and continued. "I think I'm calling for a lawyer named Edwards." Of the three names in the firm, the indecipherable signature seemed closest to that one. I hung up after a leaving a quick message. I was curious about why they wanted to contact me.

Then the scatter of neglected mail on the table in front of me came into focus, and I noticed there, hidden between a glossy flier from Jim's Shoe Emporium and an overdue electric bill, lay three letters with the official Town of Pine Grove seal in the return address area. It showed a pine tree on a lake shore in blue silhouette, with the letters P and G on either side. All three letter were addressed to me, and all of them looked important. I silently cursed myself for having ignored them until now.

Thinking back over the last couple of weeks, I vaguely remembered that I had stuffed three days' worth of bills and junk mail there two Fridays earlier. That had been the last time I went to work at the coffee shop. When I came home after quitting unceremoniously, I was distracted enough to grab the mail on my way in and stick it wherever. Then I had forgotten about it, and I hadn't checked the mailbox again since then, either.

Now I felt foolish, being a grown woman stuffing her responsibilities away like sweeping dust under the rug. Time to face the music and open the mail.

I ripped open all three envelopes quickly before reading any of the pages inside, but I could tell right away they were all the same basic letter. Printed on official Town of Pine Grove stationary, the letters were short and formal, and unfortunately vague. They mentioned only that there were "maintenance issues" and "safety concerns" regarding the upkeep of the property.

So my grandma's old house needed some repairs—easy enough. Sometimes if you let the paint chip too much, people didn't like the look of it in their neighborhood, and in small towns like Pine Grove, they might take the time to address it. Aunt Daphne had been getting older, and had probably let the place go a little—no big deal.

The envelope with the most recent date on it, however, contained a second sheet of paper that looked very official indeed. At the top of the probably fifty rows of tiny type-writer style print was the heading *Citation: Residential Code Violations*. Under that was the address I remember reading on Christmas cards sent from my grandmother: 1701 Evergreen

Circle. Then there was a list of code numbers that were offended by whatever was going on at that house. About halfway down the page was one part in particular that was confusing to me. In the field labeled *Property Owner* was *Jessica Weston*.

But how could that be? I didn't own that house. I didn't own any house. Technically, I didn't even have my name on the lease for the apartment I was living in—it was still in Charlie's name.

Surely Aunt Daphne wouldn't have left the house to me, would she? I knew my mother wouldn't want it. She moved on years ago from Pine Grove because it was what she called "just too small time, darling." The house would have passed next to my Uncle Rick—after all, it was his parents' house and his childhood home, too. But, although he was included at dinners and holidays over the years, no one in the family would ever trust him not to gamble away the family property if he had the chance. Being the only grandchild, I suppose it was possible that my aunt had considered me to be her heir.

It looked like I needed to plan a trip to Minnesota. The funeral was in less than a week, and I didn't want to miss it. I also wanted a chance to check out the house for myself. And I had been missing Pine Grove, and the connection to my family, for a long time.

There wasn't much left in Arizona for me anymore. Without Charlie, I didn't really want to stay in the apartment we had shared. And without my crappy coffee shop job, my schedule had cleared completely. Even the secondhand shops and garage sales weren't as good down here, which was one more thing I missed about Minnesota. Searching for worn whodunits to read was one of my favorite ways to spend a weekend, but it seemed like all I ever found here in Plainsborough were the same newer titles I'd already read.

I looked out the window at the sun-baked reds and browns of the desert emptiness surrounding our little suburban neighborhood. I was ready to go as soon as I could book a flight and pack my bags. Maybe a change of scenery would help me figure out what the heck I wanted to do next with my life. Charlie never understood that I wanted to find something more interesting than a time-sucking job and a suburban lifestyle. Whatever it was I was looking for to fill the void, it wasn't in Arizona.

What do you pack to visit northern Minnesota in early May? I remembered that the end of winter sometimes arrived pretty late, but it must be warm there by now. It was almost eighty degrees every day in Arizona already. Surely it would be Springtime up there, too. I didn't know how long I would stay, and I wanted to be prepared. In the end, I decided I would ship two boxes of clothes and shoes to myself with a three-day guaranteed delivery. I couldn't take much on the plane, and I didn't trust the airport with my luggage.

Being so far away from my family and home state had meant falling out of the loop, and now I was getting roped back in. My aunt had passed and her house—or my house—was in some kind of trouble. What other news had failed to reach me? It was time to go back to Pine Grove and find out what was going on.

2

FRIDAY

When the plane landed in Minnesota, it was cold. Since it was May, there were muddy puddles scattered around the edge of the small airstrip instead of piles of snow, but the air whipping past my face was frigid.

After receiving the strange invitation to my aunt's funeral, I had booked a ticket for a flight that stopped over in Minneapolis and then on to the only small airport near Pine Grove. The Mistletoe County Airport was a few miles from town and was bordered by the tall pines that gave the town its name.

I pulled my hooded sweatshirt closer around me and made a mental note to layer on another one or two sweatshirts as soon as I had the chance. But I had checked no luggage, and I only had the few pieces of clothing that I'd squeezed into the tiny regulation-size carry-on bag slung over my shoulder. The rest of my clothes, including my black

11

dress for the funeral on Saturday, I had shipped to myself from the post office back in Plainsborough before I left. I hoped the post office would keep its promise because I was going to need all the extra layers I could get.

The airport wasn't much more than a long metal rectangle beside the airstrip. At the edge of the tarmac, a man in an airport employee uniform was holding the door open and greeting everyone who arrived. At first I didn't recognize him, but then I realized it was a guy I had seen around town when we were teenagers. One of my friends back then had even dated him for a little while, though I couldn't remember his name. He was always nice to my friend, and I was about to say something when I realized he didn't remember me at all. Not that surprising. I was almost forty now, and I must look really different from when I was last in town at the age of twenty-five. I'd let my naturally brown hair grow out from its died-blond many years past, and I now wore thick glasses that were not part of my wardrobe in high school. As I entered the terminal, I smiled at him.

The inside of the modest airport terminal wasn't any warmer than the outside. I didn't remember being cold all the time while in Pine Grove when I was younger, but maybe I had just been used to it.

I caught the smell of fried food in the air, and my stomach tightened at the thought of lunch. I knew there was a little café out here, but I had never eaten there before. The delicious onion and garlicky smell led me down the wide corridor to where a large doorway opened into a wood-paneled dining room. It was bright inside, with one entire wall of full-length windows facing out onto the runway. Looking out, I saw the familiar wall of the forest all the way around. It was warmer inside the café, even with all the tall windows. I inhaled deeply and thought I caught the smell of cinnamon rolls baking on top of half a dozen other delicious scents.

"Hi, I'll be right with you," called a disembodied voice from behind the counter. A young blond woman popped out and smiled at me. "Sit anywhere you'd like." She gestured toward the four round tables that filled the main floor of the small restaurant. They were all open, and other than one man in an airport maintenance uniform seated at the lunch counter, the little diner was empty.

I chose a seat at the table closest to the windows and the server handed me a menu. After taking my drink order, she smiled at me several more times before going back into the kitchen. I pulled out my phone and double-checked the email confirmation I'd received about the UdriveMe ride I scheduled to pick me up and take me into town. I had just enough time to eat before my ride, which was scheduled to arrive at noon.

There was a blackboard that read *Soup of the Day: Reuben Chowder*, and I actually salivated imagining what might be involved in that concoction. Chowder sounded like just the sort of thing to warm me up on this chilly morning. When the waitress came back for my order, I asked her about the soup.

"You'll want to try it in the bread bowl, for sure. Let me bring you one—steaming hot," she answered.

And she was right. The thick soup was amazing in the bread bowl. Filled with tender chunks of corned beef bobbing in Swiss cheese-laden cream, it paired perfectly with the flaky bread crust that surrounded it. I gorged myself on the rich cheesy goodness, slurping openly on my spoon by the end.

When I looked at my phone again, it was already twelve-fifteen. Then I looked over my shoulder and saw a big man in a dark coat looming in the doorway to the airport terminal. He was wearing a trucker style cap over a square jaw. There was a scowl on his weathered face, and he was scowling right at me. Had my enthusiastic soup ladling offended him?

When I gave him a meek smile, he approached my table in two long strides. "You're late for your ride," was all he said, then he turned and walked out. I shot a nervous glance at my server, who shrugged apologetically from behind the counter. Then I scooped up my phone and bag and went to the register to pay for my soup.

"Where did he learn to make chowder like that?" I asked, gesturing toward the skinny guy I could see through the serving window in the kitchen.

"Oh, we don't make that soup here. It comes from the Stonehaus Deli in Pine Grove. We get a special delivery in every few days. If you liked that one, just wait until you try the Chicken Tortilla."

I thanked her and hurried out after the dark-haired grouchy guy who came from UdriveMe. When I got outside, I saw my driver was behind the wheel of an overly large pickup truck idling at the curb. I had to grab the handle on the inside of the door frame to haul myself up into the passenger seat. Not too gracefully, either. The seats were amazingly plush, and I was already sinking sleepily into mine by the time we were pulling out onto the highway, headed toward town.

"So, kind of cold for May, isn't it?" In Minnesota, as in most other places in the world, weather makes for the easiest small talk. Not with this guy, however.

"Warmer than yesterday," was all he said, in a tone that discouraged further conversation. I looked him over more closely as he glared holes through the windshield. He wasn't that tall, probably not much taller than me. But he had a stocky frame with wide shoulders and biceps as thick as maple tree trunks under his tan work jacket. As if he could feel my eyes on him, his square jaw twitched under the scruffy brown beard. Embarrassed, I glanced back out my window at the lush Minnesota scenery.

The new leaves on the branches of maples and oaks were filling in the forest around the wide pine trees, and the undergrowth was springing up from where it had rested under the winter freeze and thaw. The variety of emerald hues was mesmerizing—I'd forgotten how freeing it felt to be surrounded by life and nature instead of concrete and gravel.

Cracking the truck window, I inhaled deeply. I could smell the dampness of the freshly uncovered earth and the mint of the pine sap. Minnesota air was clean and filled with the love of its ten thousand lakes. That meant humidity, and lots of it—when the snow melted, the leaves rotted and basements flooded. But all that water made for rich soil and tall trees.

As the forest thinned and we traveled closer to town, we passed a few driveways set far apart, snaking off into the woods to private homes unseen. Before long, we were at the carved wooden sign that read *Welcome to Pine Grove,* featuring the same pine tree logo I'd recently seen on my mail. It was the same sign that I remembered from my childhood in Minnesota. When I saw that loon, I felt a wave of nostalgia that was like pulling on an old sweater. I remembered how happy I was every June when Mom drove me up here to Grandma's, and it was when I saw that sign that I knew it was time for everything to change for me until school started again.

I had enjoyed living with my mom in the nearby city of

Saint Claire just fine. I hadn't even minded how small our apartment was, though it had disappointed me when the landlord had said "no" to any type of pets. But my summers at Grandma's house were my time to live free—reading mysteries in the tall grass, dipping my bare feet in the pond's edge, and hiking down forest trails with my friends. My youth might be gone, but the magic of the north woods was still alive for me.

As we drove further into town, we went past neighborhoods of neat square houses set on perfect lawns, each covered with a different shade of tan stucco and framed by tall trees. The mid-century saplings planted in each yard had grown into new millennium monsters that threatened the very sidewalks they shaded. I hadn't realized how much I missed the rolling green lawns of the Midwest until I saw them again.

My phone vibrated in my sweatshirt pocket, and when I pulled it out, I saw it was an incoming call from a local Pine Grove number.

"Hello?"

"Yes, Mrs. Weston. This is Ms. Edwards. Thank you for calling yesterday, though I had hoped to hear from you much sooner." What kind of greeting was that? I was already in trouble and I had no idea why.

"Uh—what?" was my less-than-thought-out response.

"Yes, well. It seems we have a problem here. The 'here' in question being more specifically the residence owned until recently by one Miss Daphne Braun, at 1701 Evergreen Circle." No time for small talk when you billed by the hour. She spoke like everything she said was really official—maybe that was just a lawyer thing.

Ms. Edwards took in a pretentious breath, and I slipped

in a question. "How recently? When was she…deceased? No one called me."

"The date in question would be precisely two weeks ago yesterday. And another relative claimed to have plans to contact you regarding my client's passing. More specifically, it was a Mr. Richard Braun III."

That would be my Uncle Rick. I groaned inwardly as I remembered how unreliable he had always been in the past. I doubted if he even remembered that he had volunteered to call me after he said he would. No wonder I hadn't heard about Aunt Daphne.

"But the house is the issue of contention here. There is the matter of the dispossession and reclamation of the property by the town of Pine Grove if the cited conditions are not met, and as I'm sure you've realized by now, City Councilman Adams is not a patient individual."

Dispossession and reclamation? That sounded like they wanted to take my grandma's house, although this lady had a way of making basic things sound complicated.

"Hang on a minute. What are you talking about? What's wrong with the house?" The letters from that Councilman Adams were threatening, but not very specific. What had Daphne done to the place—burned it down? Asked to be buried in it?

The lawyer cleared her throat importantly. "It's the matter of the mess there that is in question, as your aunt, my client, was fully aware for many weeks before her passing. That she chose not to resolve the issue has only caused further citations, but I'm afraid the city cannot continue to wait, specifically Councilman Adams. The lot simply must be cleaned up."

I didn't know this Councilman Adams, but he already

sounded like a real jerk.

"As the new owner of the property, it will be your name on the citations now," she said. "So this is your problem to resolve. You must do something about this mess, and urgently." Before I had the chance to ask her any more questions, Ms. Edwards must've decided she had spent quite enough time talking to someone who wasn't paying her by the hour.

I could have sworn I saw the big guy in the driver's seat smirk a little at something he overheard.

"Good day, Mrs. Weston. I must attend to a client. I will see you soon, I expect."

Hanging up the phone, I thought over the odd conversation. I was still numb inside from the news, but it was starting to sink in.

Aunt Daphne had really left that big old house to me in her will! I was not sure if I was pleased. What could be so wrong with the place? Ms. Edwards had said the property was a mess. But a mess of what? It was a short drive through town, and soon I would see for myself.

We were approaching the downtown district, and I saw that many of the same small businesses were still in the rows of low log-fronted buildings that lined the central road running through Pine Grove. We passed the used bookstore on the left, its dark blue painted facade crowned by a red sign that read *Ruby's Bookstore*. I had treasured the Saturday afternoons spent deep in the aisles of old mysteries while my Aunt Daphne reminisced with her close friend, Ruby Reynolds. I wondered if she was still around after all these years.

After the bookstore was Pine Tree Pet and Hobby, where I spent my allowance every week until I was old enough to go to the movie theater with my friends instead. I could see bright green birds in a row of cages lined up in the store's front window. I smiled to myself when I remembered the way the huge macaw, that had been a resident there, had been wary of my aunt in her rainbow array of vintage clothing. Aunt Daphne never did see the humor in it.

Then I saw the first business downtown I didn't recognize—it was in an old two-story structure surrounded by red cedar siding and dominated by the huge stacked stone chimney that rose all the way up one side. Back in the years when I visited the town before, the place had always stood empty and was shuttered up tight. But now it looked like someone had reopened it. The wide metal plaque on the wall beside the old double doors read *Stonehaus Deli*—that must be where the tasty soup came from that I had for lunch. I made a mental note to come back here soon for more.

While we waited at the corner for a red light, I looked to the left and saw Pat's Hardware. Aunt Daphne always said Pat was no good, and that his wife Betty was "not to be trusted." Those were harsh words coming from her—I'd never heard her say anything less than kind about anyone. Then I saw Old Pat himself, coming to the door and looking around the row of parked vehicles, as if trying to find someone. When his eyes landed on me, where I was gawking at the stores from the truck window, he stopped. He gave me a sullen stare that looked a lot like the one I'd seen on my big square-jawed driver just a few minutes earlier. We locked eyes for a few seconds before he muttered something I couldn't hear and went back inside.

Surprised, I didn't look away. What had I done to get a nasty look like that from someone I hadn't seen for more than a decade? I thought about asking my silent companion if he'd noticed the interaction, but he was scowling hard at the last

19

miles between us and his destination, so I didn't bother him again. I had been in town less than an hour, and already I was getting the cold shoulder from two of the locals.

So much for Minnesota nice.

3

My silent driver and I were headed for the east edge of town. All of Pine Grove was only a few miles from end to end, and before long, we were turning onto the narrow paved road marked Evergreen Circle. After about half a mile of winding past log-built homes, separated by stands of tall pine trees, we came to the circular end that gave the road its name. There I saw the old wooden mailbox post my grandpa had built when my mom was still a kid and the letters carved into it reading *Braun*.

My mother preferred city life to this. As a kid, I never understood how she could tire of the fresh greenery and the light sound of birdsong outside the windows every morning. I was already glad to be back in the woods for a while, even if I was a little nervous about what I would find at the house. Though the lot was private, with only two neighboring houses close enough to see from this one, I knew we were all still within the larger city limits of Pine Grove. That made us subject to their laws and ordinances. But who would feel the need to complain about the property all the way out here?

As we started up the driveway, a twinkle of reflected sunlight caught my eye from underneath one of the two towering pines that stood guard on either side of the entrance. There was something red and shiny there, and not just *one* something I realized, but a bunch of them. Whatever they were, they were only the beginning of what I saw in the yard up ahead.

The fresh growth wasn't long enough to need mowing yet, but the ferns and weeds grew twice as fast as the grass, and there were knee-high sprigs of neon green sprouting up everywhere. The young plants were competing for space, however, with an army of little statue people. Pointy hats painted in bright colors perched on the heads of the fifty or more lawn gnomes scattered all around the front yard. Was that what had the Councilman all worked up? A village of concrete citizens, minding their own business? I doubted it.

The overall effect was sort of cute, although seriously overdone. She had posed the little guys doing the various tasks they were holding the tools for—a few taller gnomes with smiling faces were standing in a flower bed, each holding a shovel or pushing a wheelbarrow, and half a dozen short ones with mischievous expressions circled around a stump with axes in their tiny hands.

Then I was close enough to the house to see there was more that was new since my last visit fifteen years earlier. Much more. As the driver pulled up to park the truck in front of the three-car log-built garage, I saw there was a row of stuff piled all along the paving stones leading from there to the house. The path itself wasn't even visible anymore under whatever was piled on top of it.

I stared open-mouthed at the mess. What in the heck had

Aunt Daphne been doing here? Maybe she had been nuttier than squirrel poo after all. I knew she had always enjoyed thrift store shopping to collect old and interesting objects—I had loved the opportunities to join her. But what kind of collection could this be?

I thanked the square-faced guy for the ride and decided to leave him a tip and a favorable rating online later just to cheer him up a little. He revved the engine, powered back down the driveway, and was gone.

Slinging my carry-on bag over my shoulder, I looked up at the big house that dominated the whole cluttered scene. It was just as I knew it would be. Golden brown logs inside and out, it stood quiet and shaded by the thick stand of white pines that grew all around the yard. I wished Grandma or Aunt Daphne were still here to make it feel like home. But when I pulled the old spare key from under the rubber doormat and opened the heavy oak front door, a different sort of full house greeted me.

That was just it. The room in front of me was full—of stuff. Tons of stuff.

There was a path leading forward from the front door through what I knew had once looked like a living room. It was like someone had carved a tunnel out just wide enough for one person to pass through. Fortunately for me, that person had been Aunt Daphne, and she had not been a small woman. So there was room for about one and a half of me to pass through. I moved slowly ahead into the room, realizing I could never reach the cord hanging from the ceiling light. I left the door open behind me both for light and for safety—I might need to shoulder roll out of an avalanche.

At the far end of the living room, the walls of shelves and boxes on either side of me ended, and I saw the open double archway to the kitchen exposed ahead. I turned back and looked again at the neatly stacked square mountain I had squeezed through.

I had seen enough episodes of *Hoard-Busters* to know that most people who collected too much stuff also collected a nasty mess to go along with it. But what I found here was nothing like the sensationalized disasters on that reality television show, and actually looked clean and organized.

It looked as if Aunt Daphne had bought every vase and cookie jar that had caught her eye at a garage sale, and only made it just inside the door with it before adding it to her untamed collection. The result was something resembling the storage area of a retail establishment, with inventory ready to go. But it was other people's vintage treasures all coming in. And judging by the quantity, it couldn't all have been just from Mistletoe County. She must have been secondhand bargain shopping half way around the state to gather so many items.

I wanted a closer look at what was in all those boxes, but a noise coming from somewhere up ahead drew my attention back to the kitchen doorway. The light tapping was too quiet to be someone knocking at the back door.

Passing through the archway from what remained of the living room, I saw that Aunt Daphne had not been willing to let her obsessive collecting prevent a properly clean kitchen. There was nothing out of place from the way Grandma had kept it, and no stacked junk anywhere to be seen. I was relieved that at least she hadn't been bonkers enough to fill every room in the house, although I did not know yet what the four bedrooms might hold.

I decided I needed to talk to my mother about this situation. She had left me with a phone number where I could leave messages, but since she said it wasn't "zen" (okay with her boyfriend) to keep a phone in the "house" (aka bus), I would have to wait for her to return my call later. I found the number I had saved in my phone as "Cheryl" because as soon as I was eighteen, she had said to me, "Please, dear, I know I will always be your mother. But I miss being called Cheryl."

My call rang twice before someone picked it up during what sounded like a hurricane of noise on the other end. A deep male voice with a Polynesian accent picked up. "Porky's Saloon, what do you need?" And I almost hung up the phone. She gave me the number of a bar? I hoped that didn't mean she was drinking again. Was tequila zen? I didn't think it was.

I tried my best to follow her annoying directions. "Hello, I—can I leave a message for Cheryl? Please?" I fully expected to hear the other end slammed down in my ear, because obviously, he was busy working, and my mother was crazy.

"I suppose. She might be in here later, but no promises. Who is this?"

"This is her daughter, Jessica." I said.

"Cheryl doesn't have a daughter. Who is this, really?" the rough bartender asked.

I rolled my eyes and started again. "This is Jessica Braun, and I need to tell her…" I couldn't just leave a message about her only sister's death. That was a terrible way to receive news like that—even worse than the way I had found out. So instead I said, "Just tell her it's very important. Please have her call me back as soon as she can. Any time."

"What, on my phone? We'll see." Before I could say any more, he hung up and presumably returned to the busy scene I'd interrupted.

I hoped she would get the message and call me back. Sticking my phone in my pocket, I wondered if she would make it home in time for the funeral.

The tapping noise started again, and I decided it must be coming from outside the window above the breakfast nook at the far left end of the room. A comical cloud of dust puffed out of the burnt orange canvas of the bench as I leaned in to get a look out the window for the source of the sound. As I parted the soft floral curtains, the tapping stopped again, but I saw the culprit was sitting right outside the kitchen on the railing of the back deck.

There was a young red squirrel perched beneath a hanging bird feeder that was half full of seeds. The little guy had been trying to open it, and the tapping was the sound of the feeder knocking against the house as it swung back and forth with his failed efforts.

"You hungry, fuzzy friend?" I said, thinking that I could open the bird feeder and pour some seeds out for him if he was so desperate for a meal. But he was already skittering away across the deck as soon as he heard my voice, bushy tail bobbing nervously at the interruption. When I saw the rest of the bird feeders hanging above the deck, I gasped— there were so many they looked like the low hanging fruit of the surrounding trees. Why on Earth was my aunt have been feeding all the birds in the woods?

Then the rest of the backyard beyond the deck came into focus, and I jumped to my feet. The curtain whooshed back into place as I dashed through the kitchen and out the back door. I needed to get a better look at what I had seen through the window, and I hoped it would look different when I saw it from outside. But no such luck.

4

The real scope of Aunt Daphne's little collecting hobby was coming into focus at last. I decided the source of the town's complaints were well-founded. The wall of stuff I had seen by the garage and the mountain in the living room were only the tip of the iceberg. That crazy woman, rest her sweet soul, had filled the entire backyard with way too many lawn decorations for one house. I saw bird baths, planters, vintage metal lawn chairs, and so much more.

I looked through the trees to the left of the house, where I knew the Benson family had lived for decades. The squat blue house was just visible through the spring growth of brush. Had they been complaining about the eyesore? I didn't think it could bother them much from there. I didn't even know if the Benson family still lived there.

"Hey you! Did you come to clean up this mess?" a man yelled in my direction.

I looked to my right and saw an old man clambering

through the undergrowth from the lot on the other side of my aunt's house. At first I didn't recognize him, then I realized it was the same Mr. Peterson who, decades earlier, had stolen my Frisbee when I threw it too close to his house. He was coming toward me in what he clearly considered a great haste, but it was not a quick pace, because he was at least seventy-five years old by now. The tufts of cottony gray hair stuck around the bald top of his head matched the gray of his thick cardigan sweater. When he reached the edge of the yard, he stopped and stared at me, red-faced and breathing hard. He was waiting for me to answer his question.

I wasn't sure what to say. What would I do about this mess?

Mr. Peterson was ranting again. "Didn't Councilman Adams talk to her about it? He said he would threaten her with reclaiming the property if she didn't clean it up. Now that she's gone, we'll see who gets the last word on Evergreen Circle." He sounded pretty vindictive for a sweet old gentleman from next door.

"Now that she's gone, this is my mess, and my problem." And it looks like he might be my problem to deal with, too. This guy was pushing it, talking about my aunt like that. How about showing a little respect for the dead? "I can assure you that I will handle it, and there will be no need for any action by the councilman."

My answer must have mollified him a little because he said, "Well, it's about time someone came here and got started. I knew the day Daphne died it would be a battle to get it cleaned up. She was a stubborn woman."

He was right about that. Aunt Daphne had a mind of her own about everything she did. She never cared a bit what anyone else thought of her choices. "It's just some lawn decorations..." I looked over at the heap of bird baths and flower pot stands by the garage. "I'm sure she had her reasons. I'm sorry my aunt obviously rubbed you the wrong way, but she can't irritate you anymore, remember? Do you know what happened? No one told me anything."

Hearing the quaver of emotion in my voice, he softened a little. "You must be Cheryl's girl. I'm sorry you lost your aunt, dear. She was truly a special lady, even though she had no taste in decorating, with her yard like this. I don't really know what happened to her, only what I've heard." He looked at the house and then at me. "I know I complained about her a lot, but it's not like I had it in for her or anything." Why did he suddenly sound defensive?

Mr. Peterson and I both looked up at the sound of people walking down the driveway from the road. When they came around the side of the house, I saw it was a dark-haired woman about my age with a teenage girl beside her. They didn't seem too pleased to see Mr. Peterson talking to me, judging by the scowls they sent his way, but they walked toward us and I waved in welcome.

"Hi there. I'm Kate, and this is my daughter, Freddie." Kate gave me a warm smile and held out her hand. She was wearing nurse's scrubs, and it looked like she was on her way to work.

"Nice to meet you both. I'm Jess Braun," I said as we shook hands.

"We live over in the blue house through there, which people around here seem to know as the Benson house. When I heard Daphne's niece was in town, I wanted to come introduce myself and say hello." She gave a sidelong glance at Mr. Peterson and continued, "Don't let anyone around here scare you off. You're welcome to come by if you need anything while you're getting settled."

"I don't know if I'm really settling in. I'm just here for the funeral, and then I don't know after that." I wasn't really in a hurry to get back to Arizona, but I didn't know if I planned to stay in Pine Grove yet, either.

"Well, your aunt was a fun lady, and I'm sorry I only got to be her neighbor for one short year. We'll see you at the ceremony tomorrow night." Kate looked to Freddie, who nodded at me solemnly, her shaggy black bangs swinging in front of one eye. I noticed she was wearing a shirt that read *Pine Grove High School* on the front.

"Thanks," I said. There seemed to be something else Kate wanted to say, but I thought she may have been waiting for Mr. Peterson to leave first. I didn't know why he was still standing there glaring at me, anyway.

I turned to the crotchety gentleman and gave him my sweetest smile, and my own Minnesota nice. "I'll help solve the problem with all of this, er, stuff, as soon as I can, Mr. Peterson. Have a great day, now."

He looked a little flustered by his dismissal, even if it was sugar coated. He gathered himself, and turning on one loafer-clad heel, he stomped back to his house.

After he was out of earshot, Kate said, "Freddie, tell our new neighbor what you saw over here the other day." And she gave her daughter's arm a nudge with her own. I was curious to hear what was so important, but not for Mr. Peterson's ears.

Freddie looked at me from behind her swooping bangs and said, "Okay. Last Thursday—no, it was Wednesday—I was in our backyard and I saw a guy coming out of the window back there." She nodded toward where the master bedroom had a window that let out onto the deck.

"Are you sure they came out of the window?" I asked.

Freddie nodded again. "Yep, I'm sure. I stopped to watch what he was doing once I saw something moving over there."

"Do you know who it was?" I couldn't imagine who would come out of the bedroom. Or who would go into the house in the first place.

She looked over her shoulder as if to make sure we were alone. "I saw Mr. Peterson's big gray sweater. I heard him yell when he tripped coming out of the window. He really wasn't trying to be quiet."

I thought of Mr. Peterson and his yelling about the mess this afternoon. Would he have gone into my aunt's house? But why?

"It seemed important, is all, since the next day I heard she was, you know, passed on. I tried to tell the deputy about it, but he didn't really care." Freddie seemed to have exhausted all she had to say, because she took a step back and crossed her arms.

"There was a deputy here?" I was surprised and confused. "You know, I still don't really know what happened to her. I'm sorry to say we had lost touch over the years. Had she been ill?"

Kate looked at her daughter and then at me before answering. "She was sick, at least at the end. But up until the day she went to the hospital, she was just fine."

I thought about what could have made her health go south so quickly. "You mean she just got sick, and that was it?" I asked. Poor Aunt Daphne.

Kate shrugged nervously. I suppose I was putting her in an awkward spot, but I needed to know what had happened. "I guess so. That's what the deputy told us, anyway."

"The deputy?" I was surprised to hear that law

enforcement was involved. I assumed her death had been from natural causes—she was in her seventies after all.

"He came to the hospital and asked the doctors if they suspected foul play. He said they needed to do an autopsy because her death looked suspicious. When they brought her into the emergency room, they said she had been drinking tea with friends when she became dizzy and had severe stomach pain. There was nothing we could do for her. She was gone the next day. I'm sorry."

Was it possible that foul play was responsible for Aunt Daphne's rapid demise? I shuddered to think of it, but I knew it was a possibility. It was clear she had rubbed some people the wrong way, not least of which was Mr. Peterson. Could he have done something to her to end her junk collecting? I didn't think it likely that the sweet old woman had many enemies, but then again, sometimes small towns bred surprising conflicts.

"I think someone killed her." It was Freddie. "So does Mom. She's just trying not to scare you." What was with this girl? That was a dark thing to say. And could it be true?

Kate shushed her daughter. "Like I said, the deputy suspected her death may have been intentional. But no one knows for sure—it's still an ongoing investigation."

"Thanks for telling me. And thanks for the welcome. I feel like I'm new to the area all over again. I could use some friends in town," I said, and tried to smile, though my stomach was knotting up already with the thought of my aunt being killed.

Kate turned to go and pulled her daughter along with her. "Nice to meet you, Jess. Come on over if you need anything at all." They started walking back down the driveway.

It was refreshing to meet some friendly people in Pine Grove again. I wondered how many friends who I used to know here were still around. Maybe I would see some of them tomorrow night at Aunt Daphne's funeral. But I was not happy to hear the news about my aunt's death being suspicious. Or that someone had been breaking into her house.

Curious about Freddie's story, I walked across the deck and over to the window that led into the master bedroom. I knew it had become Aunt Daphne's room after it had been Grandma's. The window looked to be closed tightly, but when I pushed, it easily slid open a little. So it was unlocked. But that didn't mean anyone had gone through it.

I followed the ninety-degree corner to where the deck continued around the back of the house to the kitchen door. There was a second window to the same bedroom on that side, and I saw that some of the bird feeders hanging there had fallen and broken. It didn't look like the work of a tiny squirrel.

As I bent down to inspect the debris, something below the deck caught my eye. Through the crack between the old deck boards, I could just make out the shape of some kind of tool. I went to the end of the deck and down the stairs to the backyard. When I walked under the deck, the moist earth smelled of rot. I sneezed, then kicked my shoe through the moldy leaves, and uncovered the rest of a crowbar. Why was it left down here? It wasn't rusty. It didn't look like it was there through the winter snow and thaw. Could someone have dropped it here after they used it to open the window?

I pulled the crowbar out from where it lay in the bushy green leaves and looked it over. I didn't know what I was doing, really. Looking for clues? To what? All I knew was if an intruder had been in Aunt Daphne's house only days before someone killed her, I wanted to know who, as well as why.

5

My first afternoon back in Pine Grove was wearing on, and before nightfall, I wanted to see what my old bedroom looked like. I was looking forward to sleeping in the same antique brass-frame twin bed that was mine years earlier, tucked under the low-sloped log rafters in the attic.

I went back into the house, through the kitchen to the hallway. There, beside the stairway to the bedrooms upstairs, was the closed door to the master bedroom. Aunt Daphne had made the room her own after taking ownership of the house herself. Hesitating, I continued past it without looking inside—that was too personal to my aunt, and it was still too soon after her loss to intrude.

I found the dining room to differ completely from how my grandmother had kept it. Aunt Daphne had definitely decorated it in her own eclectic style. As I looked over the transformed room, the green and golden eyes of hundreds of cats met my own from every wall and shelf. She had with enormous posters of kittens in various poses hung in a variety of heavy carved and painted gold frames. The tall oak buffet on the far end of the room was the same one I remembered being there, but instead of holding the special occasion china my grandma had always displayed, the shelves were now lined with ceramic cat figurines of every size. There was even a statue of a Siamese in the corner that was as big as a small lion.

Centered in the room, the long dining table was still set as though someone were expecting dinner guests. A pink confection of layered lace replaced the red and white checked linen cloth of the past. And in front of each seat were saucers with teacups, each featuring a different bonnet-hatted kitty. It was quite the kitschy site, and I had to admit, it was as whimsical as it was off-putting.

Squeezing between the chairs at the table and the shelves of cats on the walls all around me, I went through the dining room to the stairway that led to the other bedrooms. When I saw the stairs—or what was *on* the stairs—I knew it wouldn't be easy to get to the second level of the house.

I couldn't climb up to the stairs at all yet, because Aunt Daphne had stacked every one with waist-high rows of boxes. The boxes were all closed, but many had labels. The first one read *tea cozies,* in my aunt's dainty handwriting. An entire box of tea cozies seemed like more than enough, but I was no expert on tea. Another read *jewelry boxes,* and I remembered how much Aunt Daphne had loved to find little wooden boxes for her collection when we went secondhand shopping together.

The label on the next box read *fairy lamps,* and I was so curious, I couldn't help myself. I grabbed it out of the stack and pulled it open right there on the floor in front of the stairs. I pulled out a green jade glass globe and matching glass base, wrapped in an old newspaper. Both were studded with pearly hobnails all around the outside. When I fitted them together, I saw I had a two-piece glass lamp of sorts, with a place to hold a candle inside. I imagined it would glow with a magical light from within the translucent glass when the candle was lit, and I thought I knew how it could receive a name like that. There were four more in the box, in jewel-tone colors—ruby red, iridescent blue, golden amber, and pearly white. They were beautiful, and for a moment, I understood how my aunt could have fallen in love with them.

I set the box of fairy lamps aside and took one more look at the blockade of boxes, preventing me from going up the stairs. I guessed it might take me half of tomorrow to unstack them all out of the way.

But I knew another route to the attic.

Back outside, I found the tree I was looking for, near the other side of the house. The winding oak rose above the rooftop, and had grown up close enough to the house for me to use it as a ladder. I used it to climb onto the second floor roof, where I crossed the tiles to my attic bedroom window. I had learned that as a teenager staying out past curfew—not chasing boys or trouble, just out reading mystery novels under the stars.

The old tree still looked climbable. My sneakers were up to the challenge because I was a practical-footwear kind of woman. But I was only eighteen when I made that ascent, and I was pushing forty now. I was going to try it, even though my back might be sorry for it tomorrow.

Wedging one shoe in the knot at knee height, I grabbed on to the lowest of the oak's thick branches. I hauled myself up until I could get my other foot in the rut between the next logs. Back then, this was a step I had to do in silence. But there was no one in there to hear me anymore, so I shoved my shoe in noisily and kept going. I went on like that, wedging in my shoes and pulling myself up, until I was level with the roof over the second floor, where it ran straight across the peak to the attic window. After climbing two stories, my arm muscles were burning, and my thighs were strained. I was in worse shape than I thought.

The run across the roof looked a lot more hazardous to me now than it had back then. It was only eight or ten feet across from the gutter to the attic window, and it was a wide roof with a slow pitch and plenty of grip on the roof tiles, but I still hesitated.

I was hanging there, perched in my secret tree-stairway, deciding if I wanted to risk breaking my neck, when I noticed something that didn't belong. Wedged into the gutter that ran close to my climbing tree was a ring of keys. When I reached out and pulled them loose, I saw that were at least five of what looked like regular house keys, and they were all attached to a key chain that had *Loon Lake Casino* printed on it in faded gold writing. Mr. Peterson might have been able to climb out of a ground-floor window, but there was no way he had come all the way up here and lost some keys. I stared at the window and wondered what was going on. Someone else had been up here, and I wanted to check it out.

Throwing caution to the wind, I braced my elbows on the edge of the roof while mentally preparing for a dash to the window. At the same moment, and with startling speed, the tiny red squirrel I caught raiding the bird feeder earlier came scurrying up the tree at my feet. I almost lost my footing as he startled me. The little guy ran upward without a backward glance, and I clutched white-knuckled to the nearest branch while I waited for my legs to stop shaking.

It was now or never. I considered wriggling across on

my stomach like a snake. But I wasn't a snake any more than I was a squirrel—I was a grown woman, and I was going to run across the roof like one.

Taking the total distance in a four long strides, I hoped the momentum of my forward motion would carry me through if I hurried. Plus, rushing wouldn't leave me a chance to look down.

It surprised me when I made it across without falling to my death. I was in one piece, but I was sweaty. As I slid down to a sitting position in front of the attic window, I pressed my back up against the wall. That was scary, but exhilarating. I laughed out loud. Maybe forty wouldn't feel so old after all.

Peeking in the square panes of dirty glass, I couldn't see much in the attic from here. But this window posed no challenge to entering. I popped it open and slid through the opening onto the bed below.

I coughed and waved at the cloud of dust that puffed out to greet me. The scent of old furniture and newspaper made me smile. As a kid, I had loved sleeping here, and hoped it would be the same as an adult.

The little room was awash with wide beams of sunlight. They streamed in from the window and penetrated through billowing particles of age that lit up in the afternoon light like a glittering mist. The air was warm and stale and tasted of history. I felt like my teen self again, in what had been my private world of stories and clues.

I brushed myself off and looked around. The attic looked the way I remembered it. I had half expected it to be stuffed full by Aunt Daphne—an attic seemed a better place to store junk than the living room.

The brass bed I had slept in as a kid was the same one I

had just landed on. Beneath me, a once-white afghan covered the bed. There was a row of sheet-draped furniture and birdcages along the inside wall of the room, and I saw the old globe on a wood stand that brought back fond memories. I had searched over it eagerly back then, looking for the places I read about up here. The other long wall was long ago crowded with stacked boxes and trunks of past family members, most of them from way back before Aunt Daphne's time. The ceiling sloped down at a steep angle across the narrow walkway. It was a little cramped, but it was comfortable, and it felt like home.

An old wooden crate had an old advertisement for oranges on it. I had once used it as a nightstand, and I set it close to the bed again. I pulled the afghan and sheets off to replace with fresh linens from downstairs tonight. It would be dark up here by the time I made it back up for bed, and I would need to run an extension cord for a lamp. I couldn't believe Grandma had let me use an old oil lamp up here— that seemed like an unsafe idea, even as an adult. Walking over to the staircase that collapsed down to the second level below, I bent to grab the handle on the hatch door and froze.

Someone had been up here—and recently. All around the room, everything lay under a thick layer of dust. Except here. The hatch door was clear of age and grime. I looked behind at the trail I left from the window through the room as I came in. I had already disturbed the dust a lot myself. It would be hard to find... What? What was I looking for, footprints? Yes, I was. Or fingerprints, or some sign of what an intruder would have been doing in here. Why come in the attic window, when the key to the front door had been right under the doormat outside?

I looked around for anything that seemed out of place. There, on the wall by the window, was the painting I had made when I was fifteen. The carved wooden frame around it was still the coolest frame I'd ever found. The portrait of my aunt's cat, however, looked a lot more juvenile to me now than it did twenty-five years ago.

There was a dust sheet crumpled on the floor in the corner, exposing one section of storage. I walked closer and saw that a trunk was open, with a few items scattered in disarray. It looked sort of like someone was looking at these, but was that a good enough reason to climb in the window? There was a letterman's sweater, moth-eaten, with *PGHS* on the back for Pine Grove High School. It was possibly my mother's, or one of her siblings. Reaching underneath it, I pulled out a loose photograph.

Two youthful faces smiled up at me, in faded tones of black and white. A young woman with dark lips and heavy brown curls around her face was squeezing her unblemished cheek to the face of a man about her same age. He had a crew cut and a stiff look about him, but he was beaming with pride at the camera. They were clearly in love. I turned the photo over and found an inscription: *Daphne & Mark*. The man looked a bit like my grumpy old neighbor, but it was too blurry to be sure. I stuck everything back in the box and closed it. I didn't know what it meant, but I wondered if it might connect to the keys on the roof. Or even to my aunt's death.

6

I looked out the window over the roof to the backyard. The sun was heading behind the trees. My stomach was complaining about my need to eat, so I went back into town to get something warm and cheesy for dinner. The soup from the airport was still as fresh in my mind as it had been in that bread bowl, and I wanted more. And there was only so much investigating I could do on an empty stomach.

The folding stairs slapped down hard against the seat of the red armchair underneath it. I cringed. It was a lot easier to unfold it from the second level. Walking down the steps cautiously, I hoped I wouldn't be walking into another hoard down here, too. I couldn't see much as I hopped down from the seat of the chair onto the floor. I was standing in the small family room area that was set up as a reading alcove. The cluttered living room below was visible from the balcony, and it looked even more crowded from up here.

I walked down the hallway and passed the three doors

to the three bedrooms shared by my mother and her siblings as children. I would make my way up to check out the contents of those rooms tomorrow.

First, dinner. I squeezed through the obstacle of boxes by sliding my butt unceremoniously down the banister. Luckily, it held my weight, and I scooted down until I could hop past the last stack on the bottom stair. My ankles were killing me from the landing. No more climbing or hopping for me for a while—unless I started to get myself in better shape, which I was seriously starting to consider doing.

Aunt Daphne must have had some kind of vehicle to get around in and collect like that, and I hoped that whatever it was would still work well enough to get me around town. I dusted myself off and walked back around the house to check the garage for some usable transportation.

Before I reached the door to the garage, I noticed a brown tarp draped over a large rectangular mound behind it. She probably couldn't get a car into that garage, if it looked anything like the living room. I grabbed the tarp with both hands and yanked. Ice cold rainwater dribbled down on me from the plastic cover as I uncovered one of the longest cars I'd ever seen.

The station wagon I found hidden there was one of those classic square eighties models, in candy apple red, complete with wood trim down both sides. I smiled to myself. I would travel around Pine Grove in style.

The car keys were under the driver's floor mat where I knew they would be. Aunt Daphne had a habit of losing her keys, so she had long ago started leaving all of them under the mats or rugs closest to where they would be needed. I plopped my butt down in the deep bucket seat on the driver's side and stuck the key into the ignition. I turned it with my fingers crossed. It rewarded me with a loud purr, ready to go. With my hands on the furry steering wheel cover, I checked my mirrors and started the nerve-wracking process of maneuvering back and forth. I angled the beast of a vehicle toward the driveway. The car was longer than I was used to, but it was manageable, and before long, I was on my way to dinner.

As I came around onto Main Street, I saw the Stonehaus Deli up ahead. I noticed that there were only a couple of cars parked there tonight. I found a parking space close to the front door and stepped into a warm cloud of freshly baked bread. There was no mistaking it. The yeastiness of the soft dough lifted me back to a time when Grandma would bake loaves that smelled like that every Saturday. I missed cracking open those brown-crusted gems to retrieve the melt-in-your-mouth white goo inside. That smell meant the deli would have some dinner ready.

The same blond server from the airport café met me at the counter with her winning smile. "I knew you would come looking for some more soup, but that was quick."

"Then you were right. That is absolutely why I'm here. Are you working two jobs?"

"Yep," she smiled even bigger. "Three, actually. Not a lot of tips this time of year, without the tourists, and I'm trying to save up money for a vacation somewhere warm. What can I get for you?."

"I'm hungry, and I'm chilled from climbing trees," I said. "What kind of soup do you have with lots of cheese in it?"

"How about Bacon Cheeseburger?" she asked.

"Sounds perfect. And if I'm not mistaken, it smells like there might be a fresh bread bowl back there for me, too."

I was right about the bread bowl, and while she ladled the bacon-speckled soup into it, I looked around the glass displays at the other deli goods for sale. There was a modest selection of sliced meats and cheeses inside the glass-fronted counter. But what caught my attention was in the tall rotating mirrored case where the crown jewels of desserts were displayed.

There were at least six different cheesecake slices on little silver plates, spinning slowly as they presented themselves like débutantes at the cream cheese ball. Each one was brightly colored and dripping with flavor. I felt like a kid in a candy store—I would unquestionably buy more than one.

"I will take two of those wonders home, please." Love handles be damned. I hadn't seen homemade cheesecake like that since Grandma was alive. No way was I was passing on that indulgence tonight.

I chose a table in the corner by the window where I could see out over the porch, with its hanging flower baskets. At the end of the long room there was the massive open stone fireplace that gave the house its name, and it disappointed me to see that it was unlit. I imagined this room would look amazing when its fiery glow filled the cavernous space with dancing light. Maybe I would get to see it in use someday. Fireplaces were another thing I missed about Minnesota in my years out in Arizona.

The interior of the Stonehaus was one big room, with a vaulted raw-beam ceiling and more than a dozen small tables arranged in long rows, and yellow globe lights suspended from the rough-cut rafters. It was more than comfortable, and this was the perfect place to enjoy a quiet meal.

The first spoonful of soup delivered everything it promised and more. As I paused my soup-gobbling to sip dark coffee and gaze out across the deli's porch, I saw a truck pull up beside the station wagon. A tall man in a brown leather jacket stepped out and started toward the front door of the Stonehaus. He was hard not to notice—dark hair and handsome, besides being at least six feet tall. Surely not someone I knew from the past, because I would never forget a man like that. I blushed at the idea of looking at some stranger like he was a slab of meat in the deli case. Then I saw that when he came inside, he went behind the counter and into the back of the store. So he was either robbing the place, using his Prince Charming level good looks as his only weapon, or he worked here.

I had frozen with my spoon in mid-air to stare, and now I set it down and dabbed my mouth with a napkin. After decimating my meal, it was time for me to pick up my fattening treats and head home to settle in before it was too dark to find the lights. I walked to the counter, peeking casually once or twice at where Tall and Dreamy had disappeared into the back room. I wasn't actually looking for a man, or at least I didn't think I was ready yet. It had only been six months since Charlie and I split, and I was still a little raw around the edges. But I would have been lying to myself if I'd said I wasn't a little curious about this guy.

The cheerful girl re-appeared with a bag containing two square boxes of heaven, and I saw her name tag read *Stefanie*.

"Thanks, Stefanie. This soup was even better than the first time." I said, as I accepted the cheesecake to go.

Just then, the tall guy came back out, tying an apron behind his back and looking as delicious as the soup had. He saw that I had two cake boxes, and said in a voice deep like spiced-apple cider, "I hope you and your date enjoy those."

Before I could think, I replied, "They're both for me. I don't have dates," and then blushed a darker red than the strawberry sauce on the slice in my bag. I turned and hurried out the door before I could embarrass myself any further. Why in the world had I said that? Sure, it was true, but I hadn't meant to over-share with that handsome stranger. His charms had totally knocked me off guard.

When I returned to the house, the sun was behind the trees and the gnomes worked in shadow in the yard. I made my way through the living room path with no cave-ins and went to the master bedroom, where I guessed I might find a pillow and blanket. I opened the door to the dark room, and the scent of Aunt Daphne's talcum powder was overwhelming.

Right inside the room there was a linen closet, where I found a down pillow covered by a hand-embroidered pillowcase and a well-worn patchwork quilt made by Grandma herself. I was too tired to set up in the attic tonight. That climb had really taken it out of me. And the flight, too.

I carried the bedding with me and made a nest on the bench in the breakfast nook, where I had curled up and fallen asleep reading many times in my youth. It was a much smaller space than I remembered. Laying on my side, I had the edge of the table wedged under one elbow—but it was cozy enough. I hugged the familiar patchwork quilt close to face, and before long, I was sound asleep.

A sudden sound from outside the window interrupted my slumber in the kitchen. I thought it must be the same red squirrel again, and was about to roll over and go back to sleep with the table poking into my other side, when I heard a shuffling that was too big to be made by a rodent. The noise was unmistakably human, and not too far away from where I lay in the breakfast alcove. Just enough moonlight streamed in for me to read the clock—almost midnight. A little late for a squirrel to be out raiding bird feeders, but not too late for an intruder in the neighborhood.

7

I heard someone calling my name.

"Jess? Jess!"

It sounded like it was just a kid, and I wasn't too afraid of kids. I sat up and looked out the window onto the deck, but it was dark.

"It's me, Freddie."

Freddie? "What's going on? Are you alright?" I couldn't imagine why she was at my house so late unless she was in some kind of trouble.

I heard her reach the back door and knock on it quietly. I pried myself up from my bench and straightened my robe, then went to let her in.

She ducked through the door and turned to face me, grinning beneath her long swing of bangs. Her smile was infectious, and I smiled back before I knew why.

"It's McCoy," she said. "He's back." And when Freddie

turned and held the kitchen door open behind her, a fluffy bundle of gray striped fur strutted into the room with a flick of his kinked tail.

"McCoy?! But that's impossible." I looked down at the big fur ball marching into the kitchen. There was no way that could be the same cat who'd lived here two decades earlier. Could it?

"But he would have to be..." I frowned, trying to work out the age of the McCoy that lived here when I was a teenager. Logic said this must be the next generation, but the resemblance was beyond remarkable—it was uncanny. From the gray stripes across his long hair, to the kink in his tail that bent the last inch to the left a little—this cat looked exactly like the one I had known. I reached down to scratch his head and remembered the long afternoons we had spent curled up together in my bed in the attic with a pile of books.

"I think he's hungry," Freddie said.

I agreed, but was unsure where to look for pet supplies. McCoy was more than willing to teach me, and he directed me to the cabinet under the sink with another few flicks of his tail. There I found a dish and bag of cat food as if put away there for his return. After presenting him with bowls full of food and water, I turned back to Freddie.

"Where did he come from?" I asked her. She was leaning against the counter, watching McCoy chowing contentedly.

"I heard him meowing out here, and I knew he wanted inside." She was being evasive, but I didn't know why.

"And what are you doing out so late?" I asked.

She shrugged. "My mom's at work. She does a lot of late nights at the hospital. I don't mind though. I'm seventeen now, so, you know, I'm fine."

I thought back to myself at that age, and to my own

newfound sense of freedom. Pine Grove had been the perfect place to be young. I missed those days.

McCoy had finished his late-night snack and was rubbing at my ankles. I bent down to scoop him up in my arms and it felt as if he knew me, too. Same cat or not—I loved him the same already.

"Where did he go? Does he normally run off for days at a time?" He was purring heavily and nosing into the warmth of my robe as I pet him.

"I don't really know. I haven't seen him around here for the last couple of weeks until tonight." Freddie said. "I'd better get going. My mom is off work soon, and if I'm not in the house when she gets there, she'll freak out." She gave the big kitty a goodbye scratch behind the ear.

"Thanks for helping him get home," I said. Then I realized that if this was his home, then he was now my cat. The apartment in Arizona had a rule that forbade cats, and I had often missed their fuzzy companionship. It's funny how felines had a way of working their way into people's hearts and homes when least expected.

Freddie was biting her lip like she had something else she wanted to say before she left. Was there another reason beyond McCoy returning for her to visit so late?

Eventually she said, "Do you think someone might have hurt Daphne?"

"Oh, sweetie, don't worry about that. I'm sure Pine Grove is still as safe as it ever was." That was probably true, though I didn't tell her that when I was her age, I had already helped to solve a kidnapping in the sleepy little town. Better to set her mind at ease than to scare the kid.

"Because I saw you find that crowbar under the deck..." I thought maybe she was actually here because she was frightened to be home alone. But then I realized Freddie looked more intrigued than anxious, and I wondered if she might have been reading even more mystery novels than I had.

"If you are trying to find out what happened to Daphne, I want to help." Freddie's green eyes sparkled with mischief, and I knew I had found a friend. That was indeed what I planned to do, and I could use the help of my new teenage partner-in-crime to do it.

8

SATURDAY

I spent my entire afternoon excavating the stairway. I was becoming more and more curious about what kind of 'collections' I might find in the bedrooms upstairs, and now I had McCoy to help me.

At first, I tried to sort the boxes as I moved them, between labeled or not labeled. Then later on by what was breakable or not, ultimately giving up and piling them everywhere in the end. I found my aunt's huge pink handbag I remembered her carrying during every shopping trip we went on together. She had used it until a quarter-sized hole ripped open at the seam. I also came across a glasses case, holding the horn-rimmed glasses she wore until her lenses were too thick for the frames. Under that was a small book, its red cover worn from years of love. It was my Aunt Daphne's journal—I remembered her keeping it on her dresser and reading from it when she thought she was alone.

All of her personal effects went into a separate box that I taped shut and labeled for indefinite storage in the basement —I didn't intend to throw away her memories just because she was gone.

About fifty boxes later, I was looking at a cleared stairway and a dining room table stacked full. McCoy supervised my progress until the way was cleared, then bounded lightly up ahead of me.

The old wooden planks groaned beneath my sneakered feet as I went up the stairs. The dust was thick in the corners. I wondered how long Aunt Daphne had been using the stairway as a storage room. I guessed she hadn't needed to access the rooms upstairs, since she was living alone, and had taken the main floor bedroom as her own. Maybe her age had also been a factor in her leaving the stairs unused— though she had clearly been spry enough to keep collecting and bringing things home.

Halfway up, I stopped at the landing to part the white lace curtains and look out across the cluttered lawn. What could be done with that junk? I didn't know yet. But it was looking like it would be my problem to figure it out. And I had better do it before that councilman carried out his threats, which I was pretty sure were exaggerated for some reason.

I opened the narrow wood door to the first bedroom and saw that it was still furnished as a guest room. I knew it had been Uncle Rick's room as a kid, and they had moved him out of here and into a jail cell just after his eighteenth birthday. He had never been allowed to move back in to the house, and his room looked like it was essentially unused over the last few decades. There was a pile of vintage-looking clothing on the bed, and against one wall was a mirrored dresser lined with an assortment of old perfume bottles that were still giving off a powerful scent of lilacs and roses. The room was untidy and smelled like an Avon lady, but thankfully, it was free from hoarded stuff.

I pushed aside the heavy drapes and shoved open the window. Cool May air rushed across my face and eagerly into the room. I left the door to the guest room open as I moved to the next door.

The second door led to my mother's childhood bedroom. I cracked the door an inch and peeked inside. I had never liked setting foot in there. When I did, it felt like I was intruding into her private world from before I existed. It was like a time capsule of Cheryl's high school years, with photos of smiling friends tacked up everywhere, and posters of musical stars long-since forgotten. She kept part of her youth alive in that room forever. It still looked the same, and I still didn't want to snoop in there as an adult. If my mother had enjoyed a mis-adventurous youth, I wasn't sure I wanted to know about it. I thought it was odd that she never came back and cleaned all of it out. When I had asked her about it as a kid, all she said was, "I like it just like that, so why should I change it? I may need to come home one day."

I closed the door to my mom's old bedroom and continued down the hall to the last remaining door on the second level of the house. But when I tried the doorknob, nothing happened. I pushed with my shoulder a little, but the door didn't budge. Looking more closely, I saw that although the knob had no lock like the others, someone had jammed something tight in the latch to stick it firmly shut. The door that wouldn't open was to the room that belonged to Daphne until she took over the house as her own. Maybe she had wanted it to remain closed, though I couldn't imagine why.

I continued on to the library alcove. There was the red

armchair for binge reading, and console television that I'm sure hadn't worked for decades. This was my favorite hangout as a kid. The shelves in the closet-sized depression in the wall still stood over-stuffed with mystery novels. I saw that some of them were newer paperbacks that must have been added over the years since Aunt Daphne lived alone. Perusing the shelves, I chose an early Agatha Christie and stuck it in my sweatshirt pocket for later.

I heard a car outside and went back downstairs. When I opened the front door, I saw Ms. Edwards parked in front of the garage in a shiny red SUV, and she had a young man with her who looked like an intern. When she introduced him a moment later, I found I was almost right.

Ms. Edwards was brisk and all business as usual. "Mrs. Weston. This is Samuel, my new personal assistant. He will help me set the scene as we were instructed."

Set the scene? What kind of midnight melodrama had Aunt Daphne planned?

"You know, it's kind of crowded in the house for guests. Is that what she wanted?" I asked. I knew the invitation had said the ceremony was to be held at her estate, but I didn't see how that was going to be possible.

"Specifically, the plan is to hold it out here. Didn't you know? My client requested her ceremony to be held fireside."

"Fireside? What fire?" I knew there was a fireplace in the back of the living room, but it hid under a mountain of pottery and lampshades, and I hadn't seen it in fifteen years.

"There is to be a firepit constructed in the front yard for tonight." I saw then that her assistant was holding a shovel and looking serious.

Alright, they were going to build a fire for Daphne's well-wishers to gather around while we said our last goodbyes. It was a little unconventional, but so was Aunt Daphne, and it sounded like it could make for a beautiful send-off. I decided to stay out of their way until the guests arrived.

When it was time for the ceremony to start, I was relieved to have Ms. Edwards in charge of the preparations. The lawyer informed me that every detail, from floral arrangements to the flavor of tea to be served, was being prepared according to Aunt Daphne's express intentions. My aunt had specified everything in the will that she left with Ms. Edwards months before her death.

The gravity of her loss was weighing on me as I went into the house to get myself cleaned up and ready for the dire evening ahead. My boxes of shipped clothing and shoes had not arrived on time, and the tracking info showed no helpful updates. I couldn't wear the same jeans and T-shirts to the funeral that I had packed in my carry-on, so I headed to check Aunt Daphne's closet for something that might not be too big to wear. I didn't even get the closet door open, however, before I determined that wearing a dead woman's clothes to her own funeral was beyond the pale.

I marched back out of the master bedroom and up the stairs to the stack of vintage clothing on the bed in the guest room. After picking through them for something dark and neutral, I settled on a knee-length pine green skirt and matching blouse that didn't look too worn. When I slipped the short-sleeved blouse over my head to see if it fit, I was surprised to find foamy rectangles at the top of each sleeve.

Shoulder pads.

It was an authentic eighties fashion, complete with the shoulder-squaring devices that looked like they would be virtually impossible to remove without restitching the seam. Too bad Grandma wasn't here to help—she could sew up anything in a pinch.

Oh well. I guessed I was going retro then. Both pieces fit me well enough, and I checked my reflection in the mirror mounted on the low dresser. Passable, even if it was a little dated.

Getting back into my own clothes and taking the vintage outfit with me, I went downstairs to the only bathroom in the house to take a quick shower. A cord ending in an antique glass bead hung from the ceiling light, and I pulled it to light up the room.

The shower was gone. In place of the modern-ish shower combo I had known was a pink claw-footed monster. No doubt Aunt Daphne picked up the massive antique tub somewhere secondhand, but how in the heck had she brought it into the room? The tub must weigh as much as the station wagon, and it was easily half as big.

My plans of getting ready quick flew out the window when I found the shower missing. Did I have time to try out the tub? It was only eight-thirty, and as I had no plans to help dig a pit or carry firewood, I thought I might as well sink into some relaxation in my new rose-colored bathtub before the trying night ahead of me.

I was a little nervous about the night's events. I didn't know who would come, but I imagined it could be well attended. My aunt had plenty of friends in Pine Grove. Even if she might have let a few marbles roll away at the end, she still had lived for over seven decades as a member of the community.

Where did McCoy run off to this time? He flicked his tail and headed for the back of the house when Ms. Edwards and her assistant arrived, and I hadn't seen him anywhere since then. A part of me wanted to go hide under a tablecloth or somewhere like the cat, instead of going to talk to people I hadn't seen in years. But there was another part of me that was interested to see who might show up, and what they might have to say about the last years of my aunt's life. If I tried to be observant, maybe I could learn more about who might have wanted to hurt her and why.

9

A full moon lit up the gnome-encamped yard as I stepped out into the still night air, pulling a borrowed blue cardigan tight around me. The weather was balmy, but mild, and warmer than the day before. I knew it would feel toasty around the fire once it was burning bright. Ms. Edwards' assistant had set up an oval of folding chairs around the fire area, as well as a table with a small lectern on top, which he placed at one end.

Footfalls crunched on the gravel beside me, and I saw Kate and Freddie walking over from their house for the ceremony. They greeted me, offered quiet condolences, and chose seats to one side of the freshly dug firepit. Two cars pulled up and parked in the driveway. Someone I didn't recognize stepped out of the first car, followed by someone I definitely did know in the second.

The first man was tall and thin, and wore a slick comb-over and square glasses. His suit was a size too small for him, and his tie was unfashionably narrow. Maybe the pinched expression on his face was a reaction to the discomfort of his poor wardrobe choices, or maybe he just always looked irritated like that. I was about to find out, because he was heading my way. And my Uncle Rick was following close behind him.

I stepped back and leaned against the tree trunk behind me, braced for some sort of grumpy confrontation. But the suited guy marched right past me and up to Ms. Edwards instead. He stopped in front of her where she stood nearby, talking with her assistant. The new guy was loud, and angry, and didn't seem to care who overheard him.

"Ms. Edwards, you told me this would be resolved by now!" he hissed at her. Evidently, they were acquainted.

"Calm down, Councilman. I said you should wait to see if the new owner takes action to clean up the lot before you could do anything about it. And you know my client didn't want you here tonight."

The councilman guffawed. "Your client. She's not my problem anymore, is she? I came to ask the new owner if she will sell, before I convince the town government to reclaim this place for failure to comply with repeated citations. I have business interests to think of, and this place is in the way."

"You know as well as I do that those citations are a stretch. And your business dealings are shady, at best." Ms. Edwards was unruffled and firm. "Leave now, please, or you will force me to call the deputy to remove you."

The tall man seemed to shrink a little at her chastisement. Then, under his breath, he added something I couldn't hear. And whatever it was, Ms. Edwards glared daggers at him.

He turned away from the lawyer and stomped back to his car. None of the assembled guests looked up at the odd exchange or at the man's haughty exit. But I had heard and seen enough to make me curious.

That must have been the councilman who sent the citations about the house. It sounded like he had a personal reason for threatening to take the property from Aunt Daphne, and I wasn't sure yet how to learn more about those shady business interests Ms. Edwards had mentioned. I didn't like Councilman Adams one bit, and I didn't like the way he talked about my beloved aunt at her own funeral.

Then I realized that although I saw Uncle Rick's arrival, I didn't notice where he went after hearing that argument. I wanted to talk to him before the ceremony started. He and I had never been close, but he was my only family left in the area now, so we might as well stick together.

I wandered toward the front of the house looking for his silhouette and spotted him on the porch. He had parked himself on Grandma's old hanging bench and lit up what smelled like the cheapest cigar money could buy. He looked up at me when the steps creaked under my feet, and said, "Hey, Jess," before weeping in loud heaving sobs.

"Hey, Uncle Rick," I said, as I crossed the porch to sit beside him on the bench. He sat hunched over, head in hands. I draped one arm over his back. Short and squat, he had a full head of white hair now under his ragged brown hat. After waiting for him to let his grief out, I tried to console him.

"I know you loved your sister. I'm sorry she's gone," I said. They were close as kids, but his outpouring of emotion was still surprising. I thought they had grown distant over the last couple of decades of Uncle Rick's unsavory lifestyle. "She set up this beautiful night to for us to remember her life." It was special, with the full moon filtering down through the pines. Weather like this was why people loved living in Minnesota.

He coughed and spluttered, then pulled himself together a little and replied. "Yeah. Thanks. Daphne was always my favorite sister, even though she wouldn't let me move back into the house, on account of my legal troubles. You know, I hoped your mother would be here for this. The least Cheryl could do after being away so long is come back and say goodbye to her only sister."

I wished my mom were there, too. After I left a message with that bartender, I still hadn't heard from her. I wondered if she'd received the same dark invitation I had, or if there was even mail delivery on the beach where she lived.

He wiped his bulbous nose on his tweed jacket sleeve and looked up at me. I smiled at him, and he attempted a weak smile in return. "Just let me know if you need anything, Uncle Rick. Anything I can help with, that is. We're family, and we should stick together." Sure, he had a crooked past, but we had all made mistakes. Even if I didn't have Grandma or Aunt Daphne around anymore, I would have at least an uncle in Pine Grove.

"There is one thing, Jess," he said. "Did you find my lucky blue jacket? I left some stuff here in the garage last time I went away to, you know... When I got in trouble the last time. Do you think you could get in there and look for it?"

His request sounded harmless enough, so I agreed. "Sure, Uncle Rick. I'll look for it."

That cheered him up a little, and after one more big sniff, he corked his tears enough to catch his breath. A few more people had arrived and everyone was taking their seats. "Come on. I think it's almost midnight." I half-dragged, half-led Uncle Rick down the porch steps and over to a folding chair near the lectern, where Ms. Edwards was setting out prepared note cards for the eulogy.

I found an empty seat beside Kate, and Freddie gave me a little wave from where she sat on the other side of her mother. Two of the newcomers I hadn't greeted yet were the Sexy Soup Guy and Stefanie the server. I didn't know they had been friends of my aunt too, but then she had probably loved that cheesecake as much as I had. Looking up, the Tall and Dreamy caught me staring at him, and I was glad it was too dark for him to see the blush that heated my face. He smiled at me and I looked down at the fire, feeling awkward. He was even more handsome in the fire's light, and I had no business with a man who looked that good.

Next to Stefanie sat the Ruby from Ruby's Bookstore, and her husband, Stuart. They were two of my aunt's close friends, and had attended high school together in Pine Grove. One more guest joined our circle after hopping out of a postal delivery truck parked in the yard. The mailman at Aunt Daphne's funeral? The postal worker sat down next to Stephanie, and as Ms. Edwards spoke, I saw that the poor guy was weeping into a handkerchief he produced from a jacket pocket. It looked like she made friends with everyone she crossed paths with in her life. Well, everyone except her murderer.

"Gathered friends and family. We are here tonight to celebrate the life of Daphne Marie Braun." She gave a nod to Samuel, who stepped forward to strike a match and drop it onto the pyre he had stacked in the round pit. A small flame blossomed and spread rapidly. He must have put lighter fluid on the woodpile to get it to burn so easily, because there were two-foot flames in a matter of moments. The flames danced in the gusting spring breeze, creating a flickering orange glow across the macabre gathering. A murmur of approval went around the attendees as Ms. Edwards continued to read.

"An amazing woman, beloved neighbor, and valued member of the Pine Grove community..." I wondered if Aunt Daphne had written all this about herself. The lawyer's speech continued on predictably like that for another ten minutes, and I was trying my best to pay attention while feeling the late hour catching up with me. I stifled a yawn with the back of my hand and hoped everyone would take it for a sob. I had loved my aunt, and I genuinely missed her. But I could accept that she had lived a happy life, and had moved on to a better place. Foul play may have ended her life, but that would never define her memory. McCoy appeared from nowhere beside me and shoved his warm head under my hand reassuringly, and I knew he must miss her too.

I looked around at the faces of the guests, firelight reflected on their assembled faces. I noticed that Old Pat and my square-jawed driver from the airport were both there. When I looked at them, sitting next to each other, I saw the obvious family resemblance. The one built like a brick outhouse must be Pat's son, Pat Junior — though he looked totally different from when we were teenagers. The son was staring into the fire, looking as angry as the last time I saw him. Maybe all that working out was making him grumpy — the guy was seriously muscled. The father was—I jumped back in my seat. The old guy was glaring at me again. What the heck was wrong with those two? I wondered how they knew my aunt, and why they bothered to come to the ceremony if they were so unhappy about it.

The last person seated around the fire was Mr. Peterson. His nose was red and his eyes were puffy, as though he had been crying as much over Daphne's loss as her own brother had. Could it all be an act to make him look innocent? I still suspected he was involved somehow in my aunt's death.

After Ms. Edwards finished her speech, Samuel started a play-list of nineteen-fifties jazz music on a small portable speaker linked to his phone. Then he handed out red plastic cups like a college keg party and filled each with a yellowish-brown liquid from a big glass jug.

That was too much.

"Excuse me, Samuel," I said, as he finished pouring the stuff into the cup held by a nonplussed Mr. Peterson. "What in the world did Aunt Daphne tell you to serve to us?"

I had tried to ask it privately, but my question had caught the attention of a few other ears around the fire. I heard Old Pat growl, "What is this crap? I only drink beer."

"It's a special tea blend. Entirely safe, I'm sure." Samuel gave me a nervous smile.

I returned his smile, but not his sentiments. I poured the mysterious brew out on the ground and saw Freddie and Kate do the same with theirs. I'm sure Aunt Daphne meant well, but something about "special tea" from a dead woman was giving me the creeps.

I looked around the dark yard at the gnome faces glowing where they were forever gardening with their tiny shovels. I was thinking this whole ceremony was a little weird, and I was ready to wind it up.

Ms. Edwards turned on one polished heel and walked back to where Samuel was already packing up the SUV. The guests dispersed from their places around the fire and talked in small groups or wandering back to their vehicles while Dizzy Gillespie continued a slow rhythm in the background. I couldn't blame everyone for wanting to take off. I wanted to go back in the house and go to sleep in my attic bed until noon. But I felt like I needed to be present until all the guests had left. It was an odd and short ceremony of sorts, and although it wasn't a formal funeral, it felt like a finished farewell.

Freddie was waving to me from across the firepit. When she got my attention, she pointed to where Ruby and her husband stood nearby, with their backs to the thinning group. I didn't know what Freddie wanted, but I thought she was motioning me to move closer to the couple, who huddled together, speaking to one another in hushed tones. I inched a little closer, and Freddie gave me a thumbs up. So I sidled up behind them to listen.

Ruby was gossiping with her husband. "That Councilman Adams is such a hot-head. I can't believe he had the nerve to show up at poor Daphne's funeral after everything that's happened."

"I thought everyone on Evergreen Circle was getting a nice chunk of change when that real estate deal goes through. Peterson told me they had it all worked out. What's the problem?" Stuart asked.

"No, Stuart. Not everyone was in on it. Daphne never agreed to sell to Adams. I'll bet she died cursing that shiny-headed pencil pusher from her hospital bed."

I didn't know how long I could stand there looking nonchalant, but I couldn't walk away from the story I was hearing.

Ruby continued, unaware that I wasn't just staring into the fire in mourning. "Him and that mean old Mr. Peterson, they both gave Daphne the business about giving up her house. Adams always was—"

I had leaned into Ruby by accident while trying to catch every salacious detail of their conversation. She offered her condolences once she recognized me.

"Jessica. It's been so long since I've seen you in town. I'm so sorry you lost your aunt. I know you two were close when you stayed here." She squeezed my arm with motherly affection and gave me a half smile. "She sure knew how to plan an interesting night."

"Thanks. I know you miss her too," I said. "It's good to be back here, even though it will never be the same without her." We said our goodbyes, and she turned to go.

I was excited to talk to Freddie about the story I had just overheard. Freddie was excited, too. "Do you think Ruby knows who did it?" She certainly loved a mystery.

"Maybe," I answered. "I learned that there was some kind of land deal in the works on Evergreen Circle, and that my aunt wasn't interested in selling. Councilman Adams was pretty mad at her, I guess." I didn't know if that was enough of a motive for murder, but I knew people had been killed for less. "And it gave Mr. Peterson another reason to get her out of the way besides the mess."

It was getting late, and Kate came over to retrieve her daughter and go home. "Good night, Jess." Freddie said. "I'll think about our leads, and we'll work on this case more tomorrow."

Samuel put out the fire with a bucket of sand as the rest of the guests filed away, leaving me standing beside the fading embers with my kitty. McCoy rubbed my ankles with his wet nose as a show of emotional support, and I scratched him between the ears in gratitude.

It was about time for me to talk to the authorities about Aunt Daphne's murder, and find out more about what had happened to her. I made a plan to talk to whoever was in charge of the investigation first thing the next morning.

10

I was alone at the house, and curiosity about what Uncle Rick had left in the garage was building in my mind as I sat on the porch swing, watching the embers cool in the fire. He may have tried many times to 'go straight', as he called it, but I didn't believe any old jacket could be that important. I suspected that maybe what he actually wanted was something else he had left out there.

I walked through the dewy grass, McCoy following behind me with careful steps and shaking the moisture from each paw as he went. We passed the ax-wielding gnomes where they smiled at their stump and walked over to where the driveway met the path to the house.

As I looked over the collected lawn decorations, I admired a bird bath that caught my eye. I pulled it out of the stack where it was wedged between a rusty rooster weather-vane and a sizeable piece of decorative driftwood. The bird bath had a pearly white basin mounted on a cement base carved to look like a stack of fist-sized acorns. I leaned it up to the side of the path and resolved to set it up in the yard the next day.

The small side door to the log-built garage was locked, and there was no door mat to find a hidden key under. I didn't dare open the big rolling front doors for fear of piled junk falling out and crashing into the driveway. The station wagon was parked nearby, and on a whim, I walked over to it and grabbed the keys I'd found inside.

The second key I tried in the lock turned smoothly, and when I opened the door, I found the garage wasn't full at all. I flipped the light switch on, and the cavernous three-stall space filled with fluorescent light. What I saw there was nothing like I'd imagined it might be.

Shelves line the garage walls, but they were empty — unlike the ones jammed with collectibles in the house. It looked sort of like Aunt Daphne had been setting up for something. Maybe she had planned to move all of her collections out onto these shelves. But why? To make her own personal museum? I walked to where a book sat lay open on the counter-top. I flipped to the cover and read the title:. *Starting a Thrift Store Is Easy* was not what I expected to see, but there it was—on a book that someone was recently reading here.

A thrift store!? If Aunt Daphne had been working on starting up a thrift store, that would explain a lot. I thought I might know now why the garage was set up the way it was, with shelving everywhere and banks of bright lighting. And also why she had collected such an overabundance of things and left them stacked around the house and yard. That behavior would make more sense if she had been gathering an inventory and had planned to use the garage for her store. It sounded to me like something Aunt Daphne would have loved to do.

I thought back to how much fun thrift store shopping sprees were with my aunt and grandma. It didn't surprise me that Aunt Daphne would have wanted to run a store of her own. But now that she was gone, and this was my garage... What should I do with it—follow in her footsteps and open the thrift store myself? I didn't have any better ideas for my life as it was, so it wasn't a terrible option to consider.

Taking the how-to book with me, I started back to my attic for the night. I would have time to read it tomorrow. On my way back through the garage, I noticed a navy-blue vinyl duffel bag, left stuffed full and forgotten on the garage floor. It was stuck in between open boxes of cookie jars and coffee mugs, and it looked like the kind of luggage Uncle Rick would have used. Opening it, I saw it must be his bag, because there was the thread-bare blue tweed jacket he was looking for on top. The coat was wrinkled like an accordion from its balled-up storage. I pulled it out and saw a bunch of paperback books underneath it, all with flashy neon-lettered covers. *Dream It, Be It* , and then *So You Want To Get Your Life Together.* There were at least half a dozen more like those, all of them with worn corners and scrap paper bookmarks sticking out. Well, good for him. Uncle Rick must have been working to improve himself.

Sadly, the writing on one of the bookmarks left a different taste in my mouth. The scrap floated out of the book I held and landed at my feet, and I bent to pick it up.

I frowned. It was a receipt from Pat's Hardware, for one eighteen-inch steel crowbar. Just when I thought Uncle Rick had been trying to turn his life of crime around, I find something like this.

Had my ex-convict uncle been the person breaking into

my aunt's house? He couldn't have been involved in her death, could he? I knew he had a reputation for doing despicable deeds for money, but I had never dreamed it might include murder. Sticking the receipt and jacket back in the bag, I zipped it up and carried it with me into the house, determined to question him about it the next time I saw him.

11

SUNDAY

I was rudely disturbed from my peaceful slumber under the eaves, and pulled a sweatshirt on over my pajamas and before struggling down the steps from the attic. When I reached the living room and answered the door, it surprised me to see an officer in full uniform there waiting for me. The car parked behind him in the driveway read *Mistletoe County Sheriff's Department* on the side.

"Good morning, Ma'am."

Darn, I didn't like that I was old enough to be called ma'am already. He inclined the brim of his over-sized hat toward me with one hand, like a cowboy in an old Western film.

"What is this about?" Once I was awake enough to realize that he looked to be there on official business, my mind started racing through terrible possibilities of why he had come. Was it bad news? Had someone else died? Had something happened to Charlie?

"I'm Deputy Douglas, and I need to ask you a few questions. Do you mind if we do it inside?" The deputy motioned toward the neighbor's houses on either side of us, as if to show that they might overhear our conversation from that unlikely distance.

I remembered that the living room was still almost impassable, and pulled the front door shut tighter behind me. I was grateful he hadn't seen the junk piles in there when I slipped out the door.

"The porch is fine," I answered. "What happened?" I stood with my arms crossed, waiting to hear the questions he mentioned.

"Alright. I just need to clarify a few things for my report about your aunt's death. You are Daphne's niece from Arizona. Am I right?" He checked an open notepad he held in one brown gloved hand. He read, "Jessica Weston?"

So much for my plan of marching downtown to get some information. The law appeared to have come to me first. "Yes —and no. I am Daphne's niece from Arizona, but I'm not Jessica Weston anymore."

"You mean you had one of those sex changes or somethin'?" He squinted at me through eyes narrowed in suspicion. Apparently, he didn't trust what he was seeing. His southern drawl was out of place in Pine Grove. I wondered if he was a transplant to the North, or if he was faking it. The twang did go well with his big-hatted lawman persona.

"No need to be rude. I just got divorced, and I go by Jessica Braun again now."

"I see," he said, and I wasn't sure that he did.

Already I was thinking this guy may be a couple bulbs

short of a full string.

He cleared his throat and continued, "Well, I need to know where you were two weeks ago Wednesday, ma'am."

I knew it was the real question he'd come for me to answer—he was asking me if I had an alibi for the night of my aunt's murder.

"I was in Arizona," I answered truthfully.

"Well, we'll see about that. I know you've been living here in her house. Don't you think that's a little, I don't know, suspicious?"

Did he even know how to question someone properly? I'd read enough detective stories to know that what he'd asked wasn't a useful question. He was just accusing me, and perhaps trying to rile me up. And it was working—I had had enough of the hapless deputy and his baseless accusations already. There was a real killer on the loose, and this guy was wasting time accusing me instead of catching the culprit.

"You know, Deputy, I've done nothing suspicious," I started out more assertively than I intended. "I received an invitation, and citations, and was informed that I inherited this house. Until six days ago, I was entirely unaware of my aunt's death." I was trying to make the discussion constructive. But he had other plans.

"How did you kill her from Arizona?"

He had pushed too far. I hadn't even had my coffee yet.

"I want to see the Sheriff!" I almost shouted at him. I hadn't meant to get so worked up, but I was quickly becoming irritated. It was one thing to find out that my aunt's death had been intentional. But for him to suspect me was outrageous.

The deputy made palm down calming gestures with

both hands like I was a small child having a tantrum, which I supposed I might sound like. "Now, quiet down, ma'am. You don't want to go saying something like that so loud."

"Why not?" I continued to rant. "You're the deputy, which means there is a Mistletoe County Sheriff around here someplace. And I demand to see him about this!"

Just then, a waist-high golden brown blur came barreling around the corner and up the stairs to the porch. Faced with the obstacle of the closed door in front of him, the beast paused for a moment and I saw that it was an enormous Great Dane.

It was the biggest dog I'd ever seen, and it came full speed up the steps of Grandma's porch. A moment later, the huge canine put both massive front paws on the door and pushed it open. Without hesitation, he plunged down the walkway between the stacked boxes, and I waited for the crash I expected to follow. But he was surprisingly graceful for such a large animal, and he was on a mission. He was focused on one thing—pursuing McCoy.

The cat had been resting in the living room when the monster burst in on him and started the chase. Now they were leaping in bounds through the tunnel of boxes, through the living room and into the kitchen, McCoy slipping out of his reach each time the dog lunged.

"Help! He's going to kill my kitty!" I hurried after the menagerie, hoping to rescue my new-found cat from the jaws of the beast chasing him.

"Sheriff won't hurt him none. They're old friends." The deputy had come up beside me and stood panting at my shoulder, watching the pair scamper around the kitchen. With one final bound, the great beast landed with McCoy between his huge front paws. He shoved the cat's entire head into his mouth, wolf-like fangs visible everywhere around McCoy's face. Then the dog made a gagging sound and coughed the cat's head out and began licking. He licked, and licked—soaking the poor kitty in warm dripping doggy love. Having allowed himself to be thoroughly slobbered, McCoy twitched his tail in the air and retreated to a dark corner to clean himself and repair his dignity.

They acted as though they already knew each other. And after the initial surprise wore off, I began laughing at the whole situation, and continued guffawing until I was red in the face. The deputy couldn't help but join in my amusement, as the scene had been truly farcical. I caught my breath and turned to the deputy. "Is he here with you?"

Deputy Douglas nodded. "You wanted to see the sheriff? Well, here he is."

I didn't understand. "Who? Where's the sheriff?" I asked. At the sound of his name being called again, the dog bounded toward me, long tongue lolling out the side of his drool-dripping mouth. I instinctively took a step back, even though I could see he was as harmless as he was oversized. When he reached me, he nudged my hand with his wet nose and I knew he just wanted to be scratched. Once I got the picture and petted him, his tail wagged more and more enthusiastically, and all heck broke loose again in the kitchen.

That long tail had some serious strength behind it. It was eighteen inches of swatting power, and when he unleashed that whip on my kitchen, he sent one of the little wooden chairs flying across the room.

"Sheriff, calm down. You're scaring the poor lady. Come on, sit. Here." He pointed at a spot in front of him on the kitchen floor. After what looked like a serious mental struggle, the gargantuan back-end came to rest on the floor, tail whisking back and forth like a broom.

Deputy Douglas turned to me. "If you keep calling his name like that, he's never going to calm down."

So that was it—this dog was *named* Sheriff. That was cute, but it didn't explain where the man in charge of Mistletoe County's law enforcement was. I was about to tell the deputy as much when he settled the issue for me.

"He is legally the Sheriff of Mistletoe County. I'm in charge, though—being the highest ranking human member of the team."

"How can a dog be the..." I looked at the monstrous creature again, then back at the deputy. I didn't want to say it and get Sheriff going wild again. "...the lead law man in the county?" It must be quite the story behind that. I knew small towns had their own laws—no ducks downtown on a Thursday or something—and maybe Pine Grove was no exception.

"Just know that I'm in charge of any major investigations around here. And that includes the murder of Daphne Braun." His face had changed back to business, and so had his tone. "I do need to know where you were the night someone poisoned her," he said in a low voice.

Interesting. I hadn't heard yet what had killed her—only that she had been ill. Now he'd let it slip that she was killed with some kind of poison. How terrible! Who could do such a thing to a sweet old woman?

"I..." Was I about to give him an account of my whereabouts that night? Did he seriously think I could be a suspect? Maybe I should wait and call a lawyer. I thought of the uptight Ms. Edwards and wondered if she had any experience in criminal defense. What was I saying? I would be fine. When Aunt Daphne died, I was in Arizona.

"I just flew into town on Friday. Before that, I was in Arizona. I haven't been to Pine Grove for fifteen years."

"Is there anyone who can confirm that story?" he asked.

"Yes, the airline." I tried to stay calm and tell him what I needed to get him out of my kitchen.

He squinted at me while he thought it over. "Alright. I suppose. It's just that I know she left you this house and everything in it."

Was he seriously implying that I would poison my aunt for a house full of weird old junk? "Yes, I guess she did," I said hesitantly.

"And I'll bet she left you the store then too, did she?"

I had no answer to that. I didn't know how he knew that Aunt Daphne had a store to leave to anyone. I opened my mouth and closed it again stupidly. Maybe if I let him keep talking, he would give me some more information I could use. It seemed like I was sorely lacking in the facts and updates departments.

My guess paid off. A moment later, he said, "I know she did. Because there's no way she'd have left it to that no-good brother of hers. He wouldn't know the first thing about how to run a thrift store."

"I didn't know I was inheriting the house until this week. And I only found out about the thrift store last night." It was the truth, whether he believed it or not.

The deputy was still standing in front of me waiting for an answer, his hands on his hips where his utility belt held all manner of intimidating arresting paraphernalia. I hoped he didn't plan to use any of it on me.

I opened my mouth to further protest my innocence, then thought better of saying anything more to him. Maybe my inheritance meant I did have a motive. It wasn't my fault she'd left me this house, as well as a thrift store in the works. I'd rather have my aunt back instead. All I could do was to be honest with him for the sake of his investigation, and maybe he'd be satisfied with my answers and move on to find the real culprit. There was a murderer on the loose in Pine Grove. And this guy was going to need all the help he could get to arrest the right person.

"Don't be leaving town until we settle this," he said. "I want to know I can find you here if I have any more questions." He looked at the crowded living room behind us and thought better of squeezing back through it. "I think I'll let myself out the other way. Come on, Sheriff."

As I watched, speechless, the deputy went out the back door with Sheriff close behind him. I couldn't believe he thought of me as a suspect. And I still had no clue why he had a dog for a boss. I liked the furry beast, drool and all, but I didn't think I cared much for the deputy or his methods.

I needed to get more serious about my own investigation. Deputy Douglas was way off track if I was still his best suspect. I wasn't too worried about being arrested myself, but I knew he was looking in the wrong place if he was looking at me for this crime. Where he should be looking is at that scheming Councilman Adams, and his fellow beneficiary, Mr. Peterson. If I could just prove that one or both of them had poisoned my aunt to get her out of the way, then I would be off the hook for good. I remembered what I overheard Ruby tell her husband about the Councilman's greed, and his temper. Could I look into Adams' shady business dealings, and my grumpy neighbor who supported him, without landing myself in any more trouble?

12

Since I couldn't survive on canned food and leftover cheesecake forever, I decided to do a little shopping. I revved up the wood-trimmed wagon and headed downtown for some rations.

Most of the businesses in Pine Grove were still family-owned, but not all of them. I pulled up in front of the Super Foods grocery store, and when I checked my parking job, I found the back end of the huge wagon sticking out two feet past the end of the space, its hatchback hanging almost out into the road. I'd better just be in and out as quickly as possible.

Inside, I found a cart and filled it with the essentials: frozen pizza with extra cheese, chips and cheese dip, and a tube of chocolate chip cookie dough. I dropped a bunch of bananas on top to balance out my diet and a dozen cans of meaty cat food for McCoy. No more boring dry chow for my kitty—he was getting spoiled. When I approached the first open lane, I had another blast from the past moment I hadn't expected.

"Jessie? Jessie Braun, is that you?" A short, plump woman with over-bleached hair was giving me a perfect-toothed grin from behind the register.

Running into the head cheerleader from your high school while you're in line at the grocery store is one of those clichés that actually happens sometimes in real life, just like in cornball movies. Saint Claire High School was only fifty miles away from Pine Grove, and it wasn't surprising that some people I had known there would move here. But I was a little surprised she even remembered my name.

"Yeah..." I tried to think of a way to avoid an awkward "old times" conversation with her, but I was drawing a blank. So I said, "Tanya Taylor. It has been a long time." I smiled at her weakly. We were never truly friends in school, only acquaintances—but it's funny how details like that were forgotten when reminiscences started to flow.

"What are you doing these days? You ever become a hot-shot business woman out in Colorado?" She had the state wrong, but I was impressed she remembered I'd left Saint Claire for a business major.

I softened a little toward catching up with her. "Not exactly. How about you? You look as great as ever." It wasn't totally true, but it was the right thing to say to make her day, and she grinned at me again.

"Thanks, you always were a sweetheart. I'm so sorry about your aunt passing away. I suppose that's why you're back in town." She was scanning my groceries as she talked. "I saw your uncle up at the casino, and he told me all about it."

Uncle Rick was at the casino? I was not happy to hear

that he was still gambling, and I hoped he hadn't run himself into debt with his favorite vice again. But maybe the books I'd found didn't help him after all.

"What are you going to do with that mess out at her house?" Tanya asked.

"I don't know. It's nice to be back there, but it's not the same without Aunt Daphne and my grandma there," I answered. Apparently Tanya was a fount of local knowledge, so I thought I should pump her for more information.

"What have you heard about my aunt's...you know, death? Nobody has told me much of anything." I tried to be nonchalant about my questioning.

"I do know that when Daphne was in here a couple of weeks ago, she told me she was going to start a thrift store, right there in the garage at her house," she answered.

"Yeah, I figured that out. It's kind of a fun idea," I said, hoping to learn something I didn't already know.

"Well, the neighbors weren't too happy about it. That Mr. Peterson is a nasty old piece of work. He's always yelling about something whenever he's in here, and at least once it was your aunt he was complaining about." Tanya was cramming the cat food into my reusable shopping bag, right on top of the chips. I tried not to cringe as I heard my snack being crunched to bits.

Nothing stayed private for long in small towns, and word traveled fast—especially around the grocery store frequented by the town's residents.

"But it's that uncle of yours I'd be worried about. Did you know he wanted his sister to sell the place? Probably just wanted some money to play his poker games, if you ask me. I mean no disrespect toward your family, of course."

Then Tanya turned to a topic that was more like what I

remembered of our few conversations in high school: Tanya herself. "I know if I had a chance at money like that, I would sell right away, and move out to California. I'm still working on my acting career, you know. I did a radio commercial for the pet store and everything." She was positively beaming with pride, and although it might be a bit late in life for her plans, I was happy for her, too.

"That's great news. I can't wait to see your first big movie." She handed my debit card back to me, and I had one more question for her before I left.

"Do you know anything about the land deal that was planned out there in my aunt's neighborhood?" I asked, though I knew it was a long shot.

"Not really. I don't pay attention to business stuff like that. But I do know that we were supposed to be getting a huge mall in Pine Grove. Finally." She pushed the bag of squished food toward me across the counter. "Then they never built one. But it wasn't because they couldn't get enough land for it. It was because Pine Grove is just too small, and there's not enough people in town to shop there. I just heard the news this morning—this store is a great place to keep up on current events."

No kidding. I wanted to hear more gossip, but a woman lined up behind me and Tanya needed to go back to work.

When loading my car, I didn't know where to set the grocery bag to keep it from dumping over. The back seat was huge, and even the floor in the back seat was a wide open space. The whole inside of this car was certainly enormous. In the end, I strapped the sack to the passenger seat with the antiquated seatbelt to keep it upright.

I checked my mirror and nearly peed my pants when I saw an angry face staring back at me.

"What do you think you're doing, scaring me like that?" I shouted at Old Pat for startling me. He had appeared beside the car out of nowhere. "What is your problem with me, anyway?" I was tired of being glared at without explanation. If he wanted to be mad at me, I deserved to know why.

"Just stay away from my Betty. She doesn't need any more trouble from your family." He wasn't making any sense.

But at least he was answering my question, so I tried asking a couple more. "What about my family? And who's Betty?"

Old Pat sneered back at me. Okay, so he wasn't going to be talkative after all. We stared at each other for a long moment before he spoke. I wasn't backing down, and neither was he.

"Don't act like you don't know what your aunt and her friends did to my wife," he finally said. "Betty didn't deserve to live out her days hiding in the house in shame. Those women were cruel. And I'll bet you are, too."

That was enough. I was done with this crazy. "Alright, Old Pat. Just back away from the car now, okay? I can see you're confused, so I'm just going to go..." I kicked the wagon into reverse, and he got the point and backed away.

That was beyond awkward. What was that guy's problem? I didn't know any Betty. And I couldn't imagine my aunt being cruel to anyone. But there was evidently more going on with my aunt and these old-timers than I thought.

I steered my boat of a car back to the house, taking my less-than-healthy but delicious looking passenger home with me.

13

I saw Freddie and Kate out in their front yard when I parked the car. Kate waved to me, and I walked over through the scrub brush that was growing taller every day. Another couple of weeks and it would be hard to walk right through it to visit.

They were replanting the flower boxes and cleaning up the debris left from the long Minnesota winter. "Hey, looking good," I said. And it was. Their yard looked way better than it had when the Benson family had lived there. With four kids, I guess that had left little time for gardening.

"Hi, Jess." Freddie stood up and brushed the potting soil off her jeans. "You should be careful walking through there. That brush is full of poison ivy."

I looked back at the undergrowth between the yards that I had just walked through, then down at my jeans and sneaker covered legs and feet to make sure my skin hadn't contacted the nasty plant. I had felt that itch before, and it wasn't something I wanted to experience again.

"What's up?" Kate asked me, walking over with a half-planted flower pot in her hands.

A lot had happened that morning, and I didn't know where to start. "I'm a murder suspect," I blurted out. It was still the first thing on my mind. It was not something I had been through before, and I hoped I never would again.

Freddie rolled her eyes. "But you weren't even in Minnesota when Daphne died. That's ridiculous."

I was glad to have at least one supporter. "I know. It will work out fine in the end, because I'm not guilty of anything. But the sooner we find proof that Mr. Peterson or Councilman Adams did, the sooner Deputy Douglas can clear me of suspicion."

"You met our fine deputy? What did you think?" Kate grinned at me.

"He's, uh… probably an okay guy. I'm just not sure he's up to solving a serious crime like this without a little help." I smiled back at her. "And I don't mean from the sheriff."

Freddie laughed. "Sheriff loves McCoy. I'll bet he chased the poor cat around until he got a chance to lick those kitty ears he admires so much."

"You're right. Sheriff loved McCoy with his entire mouth once he caught up to him. What a gentle giant." I was pleased to meet the furrier of the two lawmen, even if the human one wasn't the greatest.

"What's the deal with the dog being the Sheriff? There must be a great story behind that." I said. "The old Sheriff Douglas was in charge when I was here as a kid. He must have retired."

Kate answered with obvious amusement. "It is a good story, though not so good for the deputy who works for a dog." She put down the flower pot she was holding and leaned back against the house. "Deputy Douglas was the Sheriff's oldest son. The old Sheriff wanted him to start as his deputy, and then take over as Sheriff someday, like passing on the torch. He was an old-South kind of guy and believed in traditions and legacy. But the deputy—he never really took to law enforcement, and he was a constant disappointment to his father. When he died, it turned out the old man had actually named his favorite Great Dane, and the firstborn pup from each generation after, to be named as Sheriff in Mistletoe County. He even got the crooked mayor back then to sign it into a law for him. So now his son will never be more than a deputy."

"But—it's not like the dog can give him orders..." I said.

Kate laughed. "Maybe we'd all be better off if he could. No, it's only an honorary title. It was just a way for that mean old sheriff to make sure his son never forgot that his dad thought junior wasn't good enough for the job."

I wasn't sure if the truth was funny or sad. I didn't really like the deputy, but I felt a little sorry for him after learning that he would always work in his dog's shadow, as well as his father's.

"You think Mr. Peterson is guilty? I knew he was up to something when I saw him come out of that window." Freddie had that glint in her eye again that meant she was on the case.

"I don't know," I said. "I guess the land deal was another reason besides the mess in her yard. And Councilman Adams was pretty mad at her, too. Maybe they were in on it together."

McCoy turned up and began rubbing in purring circles around my ankles. He twitched his tail in greeting at Freddie, then continued on to the important feline business of sniffing anything recently moved around by humans.

"Wait, did you guys agree to sell? Your property is on Evergreen Circle—it must have been part of the deal as well."

Kate shook her head. "No way. We only moved in here a year ago, and I love living in Pine Grove."

That made me doubt the councilman's motive for getting rid of Aunt Daphne—Kate had said no to the deal, and no one had threatened or poisoned her. If what Tanya had said about the deal falling through for reasons other than a couple of neighbors refusing to sell was true, then I needed to find another motive besides money.

Freddie shrugged. "I like this place just fine, and I like this neighborhood, even without Daphne next door. I wouldn't mind staying here for a long time."

I agreed. I didn't want to sell the house that I had loved for almost four decades. "It wasn't what my aunt wanted. She told the councilman no, and it turns out that before she died, she was planning to open a thrift store," I said.

Kate's eyebrows went up in surprise. "That would explain why she collected so much of everything. She must have been planning to resell a lot. Did she have a location in mind?"

"Yep." I hitched one thumb over my shoulder. "Right there in the garage is my guess, because it's full of empty shelving."

Freddie said, "I love looking for cool stuff at thrift stores. I found these shoes at The Junk Shop in Saint Claire." She held out one high top sneaker decorated in a pastel star-burst pattern. "It's too bad there aren't any secondhand shops open in Pine Grove anymore. I heard the last one closed five years ago."

Kate added, "We make the drive to Saint Claire to shop once in a while. But it would be great to have somewhere in town to find unique stuff again."

I thought back to July Saturdays in a steaming Oldsmobile with Aunt Daphne and Grandma, going to the Deals & Steals thrift store that was open downtown. My aunt always loved secondhand shopping, or what she called "the hunt," and some of it had rubbed off on me for sure. I wished she had lived to open the store she dreamed of, too.

"Why don't you try starting a thrift store? You know, like in her memory. The way she planned it. I could help you —we could get all the awesome old junk out of those boxes in the house, and put it all out on the shelves, and make signs..." Freddie was young and it was easy for her to consider big dreams as real possibilities in life. I couldn't argue with her optimism.

Building the thrift store that Aunt Daphne envisioned would be no easy task. But what else would I do with the property and all the crazy stuff on it?

And what would I do if I went back to Arizona? Most of my own possessions, including the furniture pieces I had collected and loved in college, were still in a storage unit in Saint Claire. When I moved out west with Charlie, I left everything behind. After my divorce, I was still starting over. I needed a new home and a new job now, anyway. Staying here and trying it gave me little to lose.

"I have been considering it..." I had earned half of a college degree in business many years earlier, given up in favor of liberal arts after three semesters. But I thought I had learned enough to manage a small business if I put my mind to it.

That was the issue I had been researching and debating

myself over all morning. After my run-in with Sheriff and Deputy Douglas, I read the book I'd found in the garage. Then I checked out some business resources online and thought it looked doable. Even though college felt like another life, I thought I remembered enough of it.

"Why don't we just unpack a bunch of that stuff and see what we can find? Let's get all the boxes down to the garage and start sorting it out. It will be fun." I could see that she meant it, and I didn't have any other plans for the rest of the day.

"So much for my gardening assistant." Kate said with a wry smile. "Go ahead. I need to get cleaned up for work soon anyway. Just make sure you're home by curfew."

Freddie and McCoy followed me back to the house. I climbed the stairs to the deck and went into the kitchen to put my groceries away. I opened a new can of Paw Lickin' Chicken for McCoy's lunch, and he purred while he enjoyed it.

"Where should we start?" Freddie asked when I had finished.

I led her into view of the cat-encrusted dining room, where the boxes from the stairway were piled everywhere.

"Oh. Yeah. That is a lot of stuff, isn't it?" She walked over to a box resting on a padded pink chair seat and read the label. "Delft. Sounds German." After prying the aged box's flaps apart, she pulled out a vase decorated with an elaborate blue and white pattern. "Looks old—I like it." She stuck the vase back in the box and removed a plate showing a river scene done in the same colors.

"Very nice." I agreed. I picked up the first two boxes stacked in front of me on the table and headed for the back door. She had piqued my interest, and I was ready to do some digging and sorting. "Come on, bring those with you if you want to. The boxes labeled 'personal' can go down to the basement." That way, my aunt's private stuff that wasn't for sale would be out of the way, and eventually we could uncover and use the living room, too.

Freddie scooped up the box of blue and white pottery and followed me outside to the garage, McCoy twitching along curiously behind us. I shoved the side door open with my shoulder and we set the boxes on the counter where I'd found the book about thrift stores the night before.

"I'll go back for more while you set things out. It will be easier than it sounds—we'll just take it one box at a time." Freddie turned and went back to the house, leaving me to my unpacking.

And that's what we did for the next three hours—Freddie brought the boxes to the garage, and I unloaded them onto the shelves. Soon I had a bunch of depression glass on one rack, an assortment of decorated bakeware on another, and an entire section designated just for salt and pepper shakers. The last pair of ceramic shakers I unwrapped were a happy couple of tomatoes, each with a smiling human-like face, one with a top-hat and the other wearing an apron. They were too precious to part with, and I stuck them in my sweatshirt pocket to use in my new kitchen.

When I came to a box labeled *Feed Sacks*, I paused to admire them for a moment. The first one I pulled out was printed with little kittens wearing mittens, and the second was a deep burgundy decorated with tiny blue ribbons and roses. They had the same course-yet-soft texture that I remembered from my grandmother's dish towels, and when I unfolded the flowered fabric, I saw that it actually was a big cloth sack. It amazed me that farms had bought staples like seeds or flour in such beautiful material. I set them gently back into the box—except the one with kittens on it, which I planned to find somewhere in the living room to display and enjoy.

Next was a box of hardcover books, and I started a shelf for them. I decided books should be free for anyone who would give them a suitable home. Spreading literacy was a cause I could get behind, and I knew my Aunt Daphne would have agreed. If this was going to be my store in her memory, then I intended to make her proud.

Freddie came in with the stack of vintage clothing from upstairs. We hung them up on a rack we found in pieces and had assembled together with some effort and a little duct tape.

I didn't mind the work, and the hours flew by. The smooth feel of the hundred-year-old bone china in my hands, the intricate detail of the embroidery on the tablecloths... I could get used to a job like this.

The next time Freddie came back to the garage, an air of excitement followed her in. When I turned toward her, I saw her eyes were wide and her face was pale.

"Freddie, what in the world is going on? Are you alright?" I asked.

She tossed her bangs from her face and rested her hands on her hips. "Yep. I'm fine. But something happened."

I tried to get more of an explanation out of her. "What happened? Is someone hurt?" She was biting her lip.

"Spit it out already." I felt like she just enjoyed building the suspense.

"It's Mr. Peterson. He's dead." I felt the blood drain from my face. That was the second death in the quiet community in less than a month.

14

"I'm guessing by the look on your face that it wasn't from natural causes?" I was trying to stay calm and ask the relevant questions. A man was dead next door, and I wanted to know if something connected it to my aunt's murder.

"No. Not natural. The deputy is over there, and this time he's marking out a crime scene. I saw the flashing lights and yellow tape." Freddie picked my sweatshirt up off the chair and handed it to me.

"What—" She pulled me up from where I sat on the floor, surrounded by empty boxes.

"We're going over there," Freddie said, steering me toward the back door. Her eyes were lit up with the same excitement for sleuthing that I had seen in her when we talked about it the last time—the girl had a hunger for mystery, and I liked that.

I didn't know if we could just go gawking around at a murder scene, or even if there would be anything outside for us to see. But she swept me up in her enthusiasm and I let her pull me out the door by the shirtsleeve. I could see through the woods that there were several bright lights shining on the scene from the headlights of official vehicles.

"Yellow tape means they don't want us over there," I said. I turned to her for direction in her impromptu scheme, and saw that she was already moving through the trees, her hood pulled up over her head for cover.

Not wanting to leave her out on a limb, I scurried after her. She was following a path that only she knew. It was a trail that had worn the foliage down between the two houses, and it hadn't been there back when I was young and sneaking around these same woods.

She paused for me to catch up with her. I hissed, "What in the world are we doing out here?" This was a fun adventure, but she wasn't Nancy Drew, and there were proper authorities working over there. We couldn't just walk in and ask them about it.

"Just a little further. Come on, they won't see us. I've been out here a hundred times."

A few feet further on, we came up to a huge fallen tree trunk, turned to not much more than a hollowed log by the seasons. She put one foot on it and pulled herself over the top, landing in shadow with a small squish on the wet earth.

But she was right. In the gathering darkness, the log almost camouflaged her.

Ambling toward her while crouching low, I joined her on the mossy ground and tried to see what was happening at Mr. Peterson's house. I whispered, "How do you know he was killed?" Just because there was some serious crime over there tonight didn't mean there had been another murder.

Freddie pointed to where a slick black van sat by Mr.

Peterson's back door. We were close enough to see that there was writing on the side that read *Beavertail County Forensics*. Pine Grove and Mistletoe County were too small to have their own specialized teams and equipment—that vehicle had come from Saint Claire to lend help on a serious case.

"They don't call those guys out unless it's pretty bad." She pointed out another vehicle I hadn't noticed yet. It was a white panel van from some kind of cleaning company. A man was standing at the van's open back doors, pulling on what looked like a spacesuit, and presumably getting ready to get to work on a terrible mess inside my neighbor's house. The space-suited man pulled some equipment from his vehicle and walked to where a uniformed officer was standing at the front door, and after a moment, he was ushered inside. A sign on the van read *Crime Scene Cleaning*, and I thought she must be right that someone had murdered Mr. Peterson.

Someone was dead in there, and it had left a mess.

The uniformed man at the door was Deputy Douglas, who was standing with both thumbs stuck in his overloaded belt, watching over the scene filled with half a dozen bustling professionals. I didn't see Sheriff around, but then maybe it wasn't a good idea to bring animals to a murder scene, even if he was a fellow officer.

Just as I opened my mouth to ask Freddie what she hoped we would learn out here that would help us find Aunt Daphne's killer, a wet nose shoved itself into the back of my neck. I couldn't control the quick shriek that escaped my mouth as I jumped up and away from my hiding place. Someone, or something, had crept up behind us on the log and was attacking me from behind.

"Freddie! Look out!" There was a killer on the loose, and he could still be nearby. I was kicking myself for ever letting her drag us into this kind of danger.

But she was laughing, not running or screaming like I was. Then I saw that it was Sheriff who'd surprised me, and now he was attacking Freddie with love. He pushed his giant wet nose all over her smiling face while she scratched him behind the ears. "Good boy, Sheriff. You still know how to sniff out someone who's hiding where they shouldn't be, don't you?"

At the mention of his name, he started getting excited and his back end started wiggling. Freddie stood and moved her face out of the wag-zone just in time. The affectionate beast bounded over to me for love next, and I tried to slow my racing heart as I pet him. Maybe I should rethink this sneaking around business. It could get one of my friends hurt —or me.

Someone was yelling at us from way across the yard behind the crime scene tape. They had discovered us for sure once Sheriff caused me to jump up and yell out like that, and I saw Deputy Douglas walking straight toward us. I gulped down my rising anxiety as I realized I might be in trouble for trespassing or interfering with a crime scene or something now. And I had just given the guy another reason to suspect me. After all, I was hiding out in the woods behind the scene of the second murder. It did not make me look innocent.

"Hey! Hold on there," he called out. His out-of-place southern accent was strong tonight, like his agitation intensified it. "Just what do you think you're doing? This is a crime scene. Or maybe you already knew that." He was close enough for me to see I was receiving his squint-eyed glare again.

He hadn't noticed Freddie yet, and he directed all of his ire at me. The worst part was that he was right—I knew I shouldn't be out there. I was about to apologize and back-peddle, in hopes of get us both out of there without the back of the deputy's car.

Then I realized he was accusing me again. It was too much. "You can't go around accusing people of murder, just because they're enjoying the pleasure of an evening stroll through the woods. I've done nothing to hurt anyone." I was tired of being suspected of terrible crimes I'd had no part in.

My protest did not deter the deputy. "I most certainly can. Accusing people who look guilty is my job around here, in case you forgot. You better have a dang good reason for sneaking around the backyard of a guy who was just poisoned and stabbed a few hours ago."

Poisoned *and* stabbed? It sounded like the same killer had acted again. But whoever it was, they were becoming more dangerous.

Hands on hips, the deputy would not let this one go. Freddie stood and walked close to speak to him, and I thought I heard a snap undone on his belt.

"I don't think Jess poisoned anybody, and she definitely has done no stabbing tonight," Freddie said. "She was just out for a walk with me, and we saw a bunch of lights and people over here. So we stopped to see what all the fuss was about. We don't know any more than you do about how that antifreeze ended up in Mr. Peterson's tea."

I stared at her, dumbfounded for a moment. What antifreeze? Did she know something about the recent poisonings that I didn't?

Deputy Douglas squinted at her from under the brim of his ten-gallon hat. "I've got my eye on the two of you. Someone around here is seriously out of order. Feeding poisoned tea to old-timers isn't something I want to see again around my county." He turned back to me and continued, "If you're half as much trouble as your aunt was, before long you'll have people around here mad enough to poison you, too."

"Surely no one was that mad at Aunt Daphne—she never hurt a fly." I would not let him insult her memory while I was around.

He snorted. "Yeah, well. Keep telling yourself that. But some old grudges run deep around here, Miss Braun. Go back home now—that's enough snooping around for tonight." He turned and started back toward the crime scene, where it now looked like they were cleaning up to leave. "Sheriff, let's go, boy." The happy behemoth bounced over to his deputy, tongue lolling.

The deputy stopped and turned back a moment later. "And tell that no-good Rick that I know he's been back to the casino, and he better not be starting trouble for himself again. I hope I won't need to come pick him up and straighten him out." Deputy Douglas walked back to the crime scene with his dog, and I turned to Freddie.

I asked, "How did you know the poison was antifreeze? He confirmed it, but you already knew somehow."

Freddie crossed her arms. "You see it all the time in thriller novels. I knew that both old people must have consumed the poison without knowing it, and antifreeze tastes sweet so it's easy to hide in somebody's drink. And I knew if I suggested a couple of things, he might be slow enough not to realize he was telling us anything important. Antifreeze was a good first guess." I made a mental note not to underestimate Freddie's knowledge concerning causes of death. She really did read a lot more murder mysteries than I did.

"What was that bit about grudges?" she asked. I was still wondering about the deputy's comment, too. It could explain a possible motive if I found out what made someone hold a grudge against her. But then Old Pat was pretty upset with my aunt—maybe there was more to the story.

"I know how I might find out." I thought back to the little red book I'd found while cleaning off the stairway. If I could find that book again, I might learn something about the past that could shed light on the present.

15

As a kid, I wasn't much one for exploring the basement of my grandma's house. It was the dark dungeon of my summer fairy-tale world, where the scariest seasonal decorations lurked in spidery corners. As an adult, I still thought those jack-o'-lantern faces were creepy. But I wanted to find my aunt's diary and knew this was where I needed to look. Freddie had brought Aunt Daphne's personal boxes down here for me and stored them somewhere.

It was damp and dark. I needed a flashlight to get down the stairs. The wooden steps were old and crooked, and spaced too far apart, with nails sticking out at odd angles. A few odd flower pots and planters rested on the steps like make-shift shelving for some items Aunt Daphne had considered overflow upstairs. I stepped past a terracotta pot shaped like a bird and shined my flashlight down into it. It was a duckling, with a huge smile and a bonnet on its head. It was cute, but its cheeriness seemed out of place down here.

At the bottom of the stairs, I knew there would be a light switch. But when I got down to it, I had to move a pile of boxes to get close enough to reach. When I flipped it on, nothing happened—I was still standing in the dark. I scanned the room with my flashlight and saw that the basement looked a lot like the living room. It was full too, and it wasn't Grandma's spooky old plastic pumpkins I was looking at. It was stacks of boxes and plastic storage totes, many of them labeled in Aunt Daphne's scrolling hand. I guess I'd just doubled my new store's inventory.

Between the piles to my left, a movement caught my attention. It was just a quick flicker of shadow, but it was enough. There was something else alive down here besides me.

It wasn't McCoy. He had planted his furry backside firmly at the top of the stairs, determined to wait for me in the kitchen. He'd never liked it down here any more than I had.

"Hello? Little red squirrel?" I guessed optimistically. It didn't seem likely that he would have crawled down here, and I didn't think a rodent could've made that shadow. I had a slight phobia of mice and rats, but I had a bigger phobia of murderers.

When no one responded, it didn't reassure me I was alone. Should I dash up the stairs screaming like the young blond in a thriller movie? Tempting, but no.

I cursed myself silently for not having my phone in my pocket. But since coming back to Pine Grove, I had become accustomed to ignoring it in my new laid-back environment. I'd left it on the kitchen counter all day, where it rarely rang or buzzed at me anymore. Now I wished I had the security it brought me when it was available.

I stepped forward cautiously, the dim circle of light from my flashlight positioned in front of me like a shield. If the killer was hiding down here in wait, I was already doomed. So I choked down my rising fear and squeezed myself between two mountains of whatever Aunt Daphne had stuck down here. I pressed on, all thoughts of finding my aunt's diary forgotten for the moment. I was determined to figure out what was going on in my neighborhood.

"Hello? Is there someone down here?" I asked the darkness one more time. Would the killer answer me if he was hiding out in my basement? My knees were shaking at the thought. It might already be too late for me.

There was an answering cough from up ahead, behind a bulky rectangular shape that blocked my view. I was about to turn toward the stairs and make a run for it, and take my chances with being chased—even that might be better than being stuck down here in fear.

A human form rose from its hiding place ahead and started toward me. The face of the apparition was still in shadow, but I recognized the gray sweater. It was Mr. Peterson's gray corded cardigan—the same one Freddie saw on an intruder. I was too frightened to move or run, but not too frightened to scream. My mouth opened and I let out a shriek like someone about to be murdered, because I believed I was. The attacker was surely either Mr. Peterson's ghost, chilly enough to put on a sweater, or it was the killer who'd poisoned him tonight and then borrowed it. Either was worthy of my epic scream.

"Hey, Jess! Hang on!" The specter coming at me knew my name. Well, I was swinging a floor lamp at him anyway.

Once I'd finished screaming, I realized that I had a third choice. I didn't have to run or die—I could fight.

Some animal instinct I didn't know I possessed had kicked in, causing me to reach for the nearest loose object to hand, and position it above my shoulder like a baseball bat. Now my antique brass weapon was about to make contact with the center of whoever—or whatever—was coming at me.

"It's me, Rick!" The figure moved further into the beam of the flashlight now held in my mouth, and I set my defensive light fixture down again before I broke my uncle's ribs.

I placed one hand over my pounding heart. I couldn't believe I'd been ready to whack an intruder in my dark basement. My recent investigating might be turning me into more of a Jack Reacher than a Miss Marple.

"I can explain, Jess. I just needed somewhere to crash for a few weeks, is all." It sounded like Uncle Rick had started what my mom called 'his usual excuses.' She told me once that her brother always had a good reason for every problem he put the family through.

"Alright. That's exactly what I want you to do," I said once he trailed off. "Explain to me, please, why you are hiding in my basement in a dark corner, wearing a dead man's sweater. And why you have been coming in and out of windows here? Don't you have keys? Why act like a criminal, unless you're being a…" I didn't want to finish that sentence like an accusation, but his behavior had been pretty suspicious.

"A dead man's sweater!?" Uncle Rick hastily pulled off the offending cardigan and tossed it onto the couch like it was dead as well. "What happened?"

Now that I was closer, I saw that the large shape he'd hidden behind was an overstuffed lime green couch. That was a secondhand find I meant to come check out again sometime after I had the lights were working again in the basement.

He let his shoulders fall with a sigh. "I messed up again, Jess, but this time it's not what you think. I've been straight for five years now. You haven't been around to see it, I know, but it's the truth. Five years with no card games, I'm proud to say. I got myself a solid job and everything."

That all sounded great to me, but it obviously went off track somewhere. I knew Tanya had seen Uncle Rick at the casino by the card tables, so I told him as much. "Tanya Taylor said she saw you up at the casino."

He jumped to his feet defensively. "That's what I was telling you! I wasn't gambling. I had a great job at the casino, greeting guests. It's my own kind of therapy. Being in there, but not playing the games—it was like making the choice every day to do better. Plus, I got some of the money that I lost there over the years back on payday. But a couple of weeks ago, it all went sideways. When that job fell through, I lost my apartment in Saint Claire, and I took the first janitor job that came along." He looked at me with shame on his face. "I've been working nights cleaning at the fish stick factory, and when I'm done in the morning, I come here to sleep through the day. That's why I took that dang light bulb out," he pointed up at the dark fixture. "Your friend kept coming down here with boxes of my sister's junk, and every time she did, she turned the light on and off while I was sleeping. It was driving me crazy."

That explained why the light hadn't worked for me when I had flipped the switch, and why Uncle Rick was sleeping in the basement. But it didn't explain everything.

"But why did you take the Mr. Peterson's sweater?" I couldn't believe it was because he was a murderer.

"I didn't know whose sweater it was—I found it on the back seat of Daphne's car, and I was cold." He shrugged. "I told you—I couldn't get my lucky blue jacket. Daphne let me leave my duffel bag in the garage the last time I was here, but my key to the garage disappeared. I still don't know what happened to it."

"I think I know where your keys ended up, but I don't know why." The keys that I had found on the roof still baffled me. If they were my uncle's keys, then who else could have left them up there?

"And what was with buying that crowbar?" I asked, still trying to ease the rest of my suspicions about him.

"Daphne asked me to help her get in the house one day when she lost her keys, and I only know one way to get through locked doors when I need to. You done giving me the third degree yet?" he asked, looking sulky. I realized he'd been too ashamed of his homelessness to come to me and just ask to stay in the house. And that he had been the man who Freddie saw exiting the window. I also realized that I had offended my uncle with my suspicions.

"Uncle Rick, I don't want you to sleep down here. You are family. I'm moving you upstairs tonight, and you can sleep in your old bedroom." I remembered the girly perfume bottles arrayed on the mirrored dresser. "As soon as we clean it out a little."

"Thanks, Jess. You're the best niece ever," he beamed.

"You betcha, Uncle Rick." I was the only niece he had, but whatever.

I felt terrible about assuming the worst of him. Here he was, struggling to work and change his life, and I'd been making accusations. I planned to make it up to him if I could.

"I even have a day job for you. We're going to open a

thrift store."

With Uncle Rick's help and McCoy's tail-twitching approval, we had the guest room cleared out and my uncle moved in after a couple of hours. I now had a cat and a roommate, and I was glad to have the company. After he was settled, it was almost ten o'clock, and I was exhausted. He promised to help Freddie move everything from the living room out to the garage the next day so we could start making more space in the house now that there were two of us living in it. While my two new employees set to work, I would go back to look in the basement for my aunt's diary. I was itching to find out who might have had a grudge against her strong enough to cause her harm, and wondered if it would explain the weird stuff Old Pat had said to me at the grocery store.

I yawned and climbed up the stairs to my bed beneath the rafters. McCoy was already warming the place where I longed to rest my sore feet until morning. It was a long day, and McCoy was tuckered out, too.

Pulling the well-loved patchwork quilt up to my chin, I looked out over the roof at the stars that twinkled through the surrounding treetops. I was sure now. I intended to stay in this house full of vintage wonders, and spend my days talking to Pine Grove's familiar residents in my own thrift store.

It might not be the most profitable venture. After checking out a tin of receipts my aunt had collected, which were actually nothing more than hand-written notations of prices, it looked like she had managed to get most of her inventory at bargain prices. But I didn't know how big the market would be around here for used goods. Luckily, I had plenty of money from my divorce to last me until I figured the business side of things out.

For the first time in a long time, I'd found an opportunity that felt right. I'd spent so many years floating from job to job and getting nowhere. But one constant in my dead-end life had always been my love of shopping for secondhand treasures. The idea of being part of that world as a livelihood was beyond just appealing to me—it was a home. The only dream I had for my life, other than just to be happy, was to own a small business. I'd just never found my niche. Selling tea cups and trinkets to fellow treasure hunters sounded like just the thing to make each day enjoyable, and I thought I would give it a chance.

16

MONDAY

"Jessie! Breakfast!"

I woke up and stretched out dreamily on my warm bed. McCoy jumped down to the attic floor and squeaked a greeting up into my face.

"I'm hungry too, buddy. Let's go." I followed him down to the kitchen where I found my Uncle Rick cooking breakfast. He was wearing my grandma's apron that read *Free Cookies and Hugs*, and flipping a pancake in the air with a spatula when I walked into the room. My entrance caused him to look up and miss the pancake's return journey to the pan. It landed with a flop on the tiled floor, and he gave me a weak smile.

"You can have the next one. There's scrambled eggs too."

"With cheese?" I asked.

"Of course. And bacon." He was proud of his efforts, and

I was proud of him, too. And grateful.

"Thanks, Uncle Rick. That sounds great." I sat down on the bench in the breakfast nook with the plate he handed me and watched as McCoy daintily devoured the fallen pancake from the floor.

Freddie knocked at the back door, and Uncle Rick let her in.

"Hey, guys. My mom's working a double shift at the hospital today, so I came to get to work. Come on boss, after breakfast we're going to set up your inventory." She was ready to go, and I was pleased. But I had something else to take care of first.

"You two will have to get started without me. I want to find Aunt Daphne's diary and see if there's anything in there that will help us catch a murderer. As the newest resident of Pine Grove, and a new member of the small business community as well, I intend to make my town a safe place again."

Uncle Rick set a steaming cup of coffee in front of me, and I thanked him whole-heartedly as I gulped down half of it.

"Will do, Jess. Freddie and me will get it done," he said, and she nodded at him in agreement.

After we ate, I headed to the basement to find the box of Aunt Daphne's personal items I'd packed up the day of her funeral. I remembered dropping the little red book into it before taping it shut, and Freddie had taken all the boxes marked *Daphne: Personal* down to the basement for me.

I didn't need to search for long. The box I needed was on top of a stack at the bottom of the stairs. When I opened the box, I caught the scent of my Aunt Daphne's familiar sweet perfume. It tugged at my heart to think that the person who had hurt her was still out there somewhere, while she was gone from Pine Grove forever. I hoped that the diary in that box would be the right place to start if I wanted to make sure her killer was locked away for good.

I removed the red leather-bound diary from the box. It looked like the same one I remembered seeing my aunt reading over the years, curled up in the library alcove's threadbare armchair.

Opening the cover, I saw an inscription on the otherwise blank first page. It was handwritten in pencil lead, faded and smeared by age, and I had to squint to make out the words.

For my dearest friend Daphne. Best Wishes on Your Birthday -
Ruby.

So it was the diary I was looking for. I closed it again and sat holding it for a long moment, considering if I should pry into her most personal thoughts and feelings. On the one hand, I didn't like the idea of treading where I'm sure she expected no one to go. But if her diary held the history I needed to find the true motive behind her murder, and maybe Mr. Peterson's murder as well, then I didn't know if I could learn it any other way.

Flipping open to the start of Aunt Daphne's first entry in the little book, I began reading with caution. If the stories she recorded here became too juicy, I would stop reading and put it down. There was no date at the top of the first page, but the handwriting was rounded and girly—like my aunt's script on the box labels, but in a more juvenile style. It was hard to picture the woman I'd known as a teen herself.

Dear Diary,

Aunt Daphne had started the entry in the classic fashion.

Today was my sixteenth birthday, and my best friend Ruby
gave me this book at school. Now I can write down all the

reasons I love Chad Grafton…

Well, that was a surprise. From what I'd gleaned from my mother's stories about growing up, my Aunt Daphne hadn't been the type to have a lot of boyfriends. After finding the photograph of her with Mr. Peterson too, it looked like she had at least two suitors after all. But I supposed even the most awkward of wall flowers probably went boy crazy at least once in their adolescence.

That entry wasn't what I was looking for though, so I flipped forward a few pages and tried again.

On Saturday night, I went down to the movies with Ruby and her boyfriend, and I thought I'd be a third wheel all night. But when we got seats, I saw that Mark Peterson was there. He's just so tall and dreamy…

I rolled my eyes. I was about to flip ahead and try one more entry before giving up, when another name on the page caught my attention. I skipped ahead in the story to the part that interested me.

…Ruby's boyfriend said Mark was no good, and that I shouldn't get mixed up with him because I could never trust a draft-dodger like that. Ruby said Pat's going to open a hardware store right here in Pine Grove as soon as he gets back from serving in Vietnam.

Old Pat had been Ruby's boyfriend in high school? I thought her husband Stuart had been Ruby's high school sweetheart. I was quickly being drawn into the teen drama I'd discovered in the little book.

McCoy hopped up into my lap and settled in for a nap. His eyes closed, and he purred fiercely. I hugged his warmth close to my sweatshirt with one arm and continued on to the next entry. This time, my aunt's handwriting became stiff and cramped, where before it had been curly and flowing.

Something happened to Mark, and I think it was Pat. He's hurt bad.

I felt a chill raise the hairs on the back of my neck and pulled my sweatshirt hood up over my head and hugged my kitty tighter.

I thought Pat had been jealous of Ruby talking to Mark Peterson, but I was wrong—it was me he was mad at. He cornered me on the sidewalk by my house, and said I belonged with him, not with Mark. I've never seen anyone look so angry. Then he found Mark, and...

What I was reading was shocking. Old Pat had been in love with my Aunt Daphne, and had not only been jealous, but angry with her refusal. I wondered if his feelings for her had ever cooled, or if he might have held a flame for her all those years.

And she had feared him when he confronted her about it. Was Old Pat a dangerous man?

Closing the diary with trembling hands, I knew I'd found a lead that might help explain the murders. I slipped the little book in my pocket, and setting McCoy gently back into the warm chair to nap, I headed for Ruby's Bookstore.

17

Ruby sighed and passed me a steaming cup of earl gray. I sniffed it nonchalantly as she sat herself down across the square table from me in the reading room at Ruby's Bookstore. Not that I thought she might have slipped antifreeze into it, but I thought someone might still try to poison her, but if what I'd read in that diary was any sign of how deep the grudges ran in this town, then Ruby very well could be next on the murderer's list.

"So. It's great to see you, of course, Jess. But why did you really come here today, if not for books? I doubt you came just to visit," Ruby said.

I smiled. She had an incredible selection of paperback mysteries in her store, and I genuinely enjoyed catching up with her. Ruby had always been a kind friend to my aunt and to me. The summer when I was fifteen I even helped to clear her husband, Stuart, when he was framed him for a kidnapping he had no part in. But I was here now to ask her about a much older story.

"Ruby," I started, then was unsure how to continue. I didn't know if I was breaking open old wounds for her as well. "It's about my aunt."

"What, you mean your investigation into who killed Daphne?" she asked.

Her question surprised me. "How did you know about that?"

Ruby made the sort of clucking sound that old ladies made at younger people who asked obvious questions. "You're in Pine Grove, remember? People talk about people. You should know—I heard you even questioned your own uncle, just because of some rumors."

I didn't want to tell her it wasn't just rumors. There had been clues that led me to find Uncle Rick in the basement, as well as speculation.

But I wasn't sure yet if I had any substantial evidence to back up the new suspicions that I was forming. What I needed next was some history.

"I'm talking about back when you were, you know... young together. The summer after all of you graduated from high school. Mr. Peterson and my Aunt Daphne were friends, and something happened with Old Pat that terrified her."

She nodded, leaning forward until her long string of beads tapped against the saucer as she set it back down on the table. "I'll never forget that summer. We certainly thought we were all grown up—we were free of school, and the world was our oyster." A smile creased her face. She was looking at a time only she could see in her mind, revisiting old memories like flipping yellowed pages in a scrapbook.

But then the smile turned to a frown. She looked back to me, fear in her eyes. "But then things went bad between Old

Pat and Mark Peterson, rest his soul. It was never the same between our merry band of friends after that. By the time fall came around, Daphne, Stu and I headed off to college in St. Claire. And of course Mark, well... After Old Pat attacked him, he was never the same." Ruby steadied herself, and I held my breath, waiting for more.

"Mark Peterson stayed in Pine Grove and went to work for his dad at the bait shop, and when I moved back to town with Stu after college, we all just sort of went on as though nothing had happened. Everyone except Old Pat and his new wife, that is."

I lifted my tea cup warily, taking tiny sips. It was still too hot, but I was too fixed in her story to put it down.

"Then what? What did Old Pat do?" I prompted. "And by new wife, do you mean Betty?"

Ruby put her own cup to her lips and downed the boiling-hot liquid in three big gulps, not even seeming to notice the temperature. She went on with her tale, growing more animated as she came to the juiciest part.

"Well. Pat was still hopping mad. At Mark, of course, and at Daphne. He said she shared the blame for Pat hurting Mark, because she never did let Pat have a chance with her. But who could blame her for rejecting him? Once I saw how mad he got, and then when he injured Mark... We just went on with our lives and tried to avoid him. Especially Daphne."

I vaguely remembered hearing pieces of those stories at the dinner table, told between grown-ups and tuned out by my bored young ears. But I knew she was right—sometimes old grudges died hard.

"Daphne never wanted to talk about it. She and I watched Old Pat go on and marry Betty Wilcox, and Betty walked around town like she thought she was really something for it. Daphne and I knew the truth, of course, and we never let Betty act too proud of herself without putting her in her place. I mean, that girl was a pig farmer's daughter. So what if she married a man with a hardware store? I wasn't impressed, and neither was your aunt or anyone else."

That whole story sounded like one part explanation for Old Pat hurting Daphne, and two parts old lady crazy-talk. She was still going.

"… Until she was starting on that thrift store idea of hers. Then she told me she decided it was time to tell the town the truth about what happened. She said she talked to Mark about it, and they were going to come out together and tell everyone the complete story. Of course, they went and got themselves poisoned before they could do it. What she was doing having coffee with that scary old coot after all he's done was beyond me."

"Which old coot? Do you know who's poisoning people, Ruby?" I hesitated to add that based on what I had just learned from her story, I thought she may very well be next.

"Your Aunt Daphne told me she was going out to Old Pat's house on Lake Sumac for tea, and asked me to join her. She wanted to bury the hatchet, and apologize for the way she'd treated his wife all those years, too. She was just going to patch things up, or smooth things out, or something like that. But I told her that wasn't a good idea. Then by the end of that day she was in the hospital, and another day later she was gone."

Ruby stared down into her empty cup and I realized she was fighting tears. She'd loved my aunt as much as I had, and she evidently harbored some feelings of guilt for letting her friend meet alone with an old foe.

"It's not your fault, Ruby. You couldn't have expected it would turn out that way. Did you tell the deputy about it?"

She shrugged. "Of course I did, dear. But if you've met Deputy Douglas, and I know you have—then you know how dim-witted that boy can be." The deputy was a boy no longer, but dim-witted, I could agree he still was. "He didn't give a squirrel's toe what I had to say, if he was even listening. I might have been better off talking to Sheriff about it."

I set my teacup down on the saucer in front of me with a determined clank of china on china that caused Ruby to flinch.

"Ruby. Can you give me directions to Old Pat's house?" I asked as I stood to leave.

A plan was forming in my mind, though I knew it was a long shot. And risky too. I would need to take my teen sleuth and my ex-convict uncle with me to make it work. As much as I didn't want to put them in danger, I would need help for what I was scheming. If Ruby believed someone had poisoned my aunt during her visit to Lake Sumac, and the deputy hadn't checked out the lead, then maybe we could find proof that Old Pat had poisoned Aunt Daphne—and Mr. Peterson as well.

A thought occurred to me, and I turned back to her from the doorway. "Ruby, be careful with your tea. The killer is using antifreeze. I think both victims drank it in their tea voluntarily because it's sweet enough they didn't notice it. You very well could be next." I didn't know if I wanted to scare her or not—whatever it took to keep her safe.

"Don't worry, Jessie. I drink my tea black. No one's slipping that one past me." She smiled wistfully, and I left the bookstore to get ready for the night's adventure.

18

Old Pat's house on Lake Sumac was twenty miles outside of Pine Grove. It was still in Mistletoe County, but it was a long twisting trek down unpaved country roads to reach it. Lake Sumac was named for the flowering plants that grew in thick patches around the area, but as I turned onto the private drive that led to the half a dozen houses that were all on lake-front property, it was more of the usual towering pines that surrounded us.

Freddie sat beside me in the passenger seat of the station wagon, searching and scrolling on her phone with quick fingers. "It says here that Old Pat's address is 1286. That must be right up here on the left somewhere." In black leggings, a black turtleneck shirt, and a black stocking cap, she looked like a cartoon cat burglar. The pastel high-top sneakers she wore were the only thing that didn't fit the outfit designed for nighttime camouflage.

"What about flashlights? It's dark out here tonight."

Uncle Rick was riding on the spacious back bench seat. He held the backpack I had stuffed full of the supplies I thought we would need for our intended reconnaissance.

He was right about the dark night. The moon was still almost full, but clouds had blown in through the afternoon, blocking out the moon and stars almost entirely and bringing warm gusts of humidity with it. I hoped there wouldn't be a thunderstorm tonight.

I turned onto the driveway numbered *1286* on an otherwise unmarked mailbox. "You sure this is it?" I asked Freddie. It was almost ten o'clock, and I didn't want to get it wrong and show up at some stranger's house as black-clad intruders.

"I can get up to five years for trespassing, you know, with my record. We better not get caught."

Uncle Rick was right. If the deputy arrested us tonight, instead of Old Pat, my uncle's bid for restarting his life would be over.

"We'll be fine. As long as we're quiet and keep the flashlights covered, no one will know we're there. We're not even going close to the house."

I didn't have much of a plan—I just wanted to snoop around. If someone had poisoned my aunt out here, maybe I could find some kind of evidence. Pulling the car off of the driveway before we were in sight of the house, I parked in between some small trees. We all hopped out and I said, "Follow me." Whatever we found out here, I wanted us to stick together while we searched.

The three of us crept down the dirt driveway, none of us daring to speak. The deafening song of a thousand crickets drowned out the crunch of gravel underneath our feet. Good —that will help cover any noises we might make. I wanted to avoid a face-to-face confrontation with the killer tonight if I could.

When we got down the long drive to where the trees thinned to lawn, I stayed close to the edge of the clearing. My accomplices followed single-file behind me. We skirted the open yard, heading around the house.

The lake lay in peace a hundred feet away down the sloping yard. Waves rippled the inky surface and crested silently on the sand.

There was a garden shed up ahead, and I decided it was a decent place to re-group. I didn't know what I'd expected to find by wandering around out here. I didn't have investigative training or know how to follow the forensics—I was just a crazy lady who dragged her friends out to a secluded murderer's house, and I was ready to give in and admit it to them.

Reaching the door of the shed with no complications, I tested it, and was relieved when the knob turned easily. I pulled the two of them inside with me and swung the shed door closed behind us.

"Did you see that!?" Freddie was excited.

"See what?" I asked. I looked around the inside of the shed that was our temporary hiding place. In the beam from my flashlight I saw the usual lawn and garden equipment hanging on the side walls, and a workbench along the back wall.

"The sumac!" Freddie said, as if it should be obvious.

Uncle Rick narrowed his eyes in concentration for a moment before speaking. "You mean that white-flowered sumac, not the red-berried kind? Dang it, girl—maybe you have learned something in all those books." He turned to me and said, "She's right, Jess. That's some of the poison sumac over there." He was pointing at the surface of the workbench that was littered with leaves and stems.

I was still nonplussed by their conversation. The lake was named for the pointy three-leaved plant. I knew it grew red berries, and that people sometimes picked around Mistletoe County to brew into sumac tea, known for its alleged health benefits. "We're on Lake Sumac..."

Freddie was shaking her head in frustration while digging through the backpack. She produced the burgundy feed sack with the blue flowers I'd found in my aunt's collection. "That's the other sumac. I'm talking about the poison variety. Most people think it's just like poison ivy—an itchy nuisance. But poison sumac can do more than make you itchy. If someone brewed the wrong sumac into the tea... It would look like tea leaves, but it would be deadly. You did it, Jess! You found the proof we needed."

"It wasn't antifreeze? I thought the deputy confirmed it." I was trying to catch up with her new conclusions.

Uncle Rick shook his head. "Didn't you know? They changed that sweet flavor of antifreeze years ago. Too many accidents and murders. Now it tastes like poison, like most anything else that can kill you. And that deputy doesn't know it's raining until he gets wet."

Now I understood how my aunt was given poison to drink without tasting it—she drank the sumac tea. And I knew we'd found the proof of Old Pat's guilt in his gardening shed. There was no reason for someone to collect and prepare the poison variety of the sumac leaves, unless they intended harm. I opened my mouth to tell her that my achievement had been accomplished by accident, but I closed it again. I didn't want to ruin the moment.

Uncle Rick took the cloth bag from Freddie and was busy

stuffing the evidence into it.

"Don't you need gloves!?" He was touching the toxic plant with his bare hands, and I could already see his skin reddening where it came in contact with the residue. There were enough of the leaves and stems to fill most of the old sack.

"No time for that, Jess. We're hiding out in a murderer's shed, discussing his guilt. We gotta go."

I couldn't argue with his logic. Turning to open the shed door again and make a hasty but silent retreat the way we had come, I heard a resounding clang on the floor behind me. I was so shocked, I half-lunged, half-fell out of the shed onto the dewy lawn. Looking behind me, I saw I'd knocked over a stack of empty terracotta pots that were now scattered on the shed floor in pieces.

So much for stealth.

"What's going on?" A man called. "What are you doing out here? This is my property, and if I see ya, I'll shoot ya."

It was Old Pat, standing by the back door of his house. He had come out quietly, and stood there in his undershirt and boxers as though he was in bed when he heard us. And he was holding a shotgun like he knew how to use it.

"You got any bright ideas?" Uncle Rick whispered to Freddie and me, where we stood frozen beside him with our hands raised in surrender. He had switched on a floodlight mounted on the house when he came out, and it bathed us like suspects caught in a police searchlight.

I didn't know what to do. So I tried using a little charm.

"Hi there, Old Pat. Sorry if we startled you. It's me, Jessie Braun, with my uncle, and a neighbor kid." I was working fast to come up with a plausible excuse for our presence in his yard so late that would keep him from using that gun on us.

"You know, it's the funniest thing." Freddie jumped in to help save the situation. "That old car of Daphne's is so unreliable. We were just out at the public beach down the road tonight, and that wagon just won't start."

"Yeah," Uncle Rick added. I was glad to see he had at least pulled up his black ski mask from over his face before speaking. "We need help. With the car."

I didn't think their ad-lib story sounded likely, and apparently Old Pat agreed with my appraisal.

"Nah, I don't think so. You're dressed like hoodlums. You're here to steal something." The old man's eyes rested on the flowered feed sack my uncle was holding. "What's in the bag?" No one volunteered an answer, so he continued. "You with those kids who raid my barn for sheep meds? When my boy gets back from the hardware store with my truck, I'm going to load you all in the back of it, and—hey, don't you know that's the poison sumac?! Knock it off!"

With no clear exit strategy available, and our plan of remaining undetected having flown out the window, my Uncle Rick had improvised. He reached into the sack with one reddening hand and removed some clumps of the little white flowers from the workbench. He was now hurling them at Old Pat's exposed arms and legs.

The old man hopped from bare foot to bare foot, narrowly avoiding the onslaught of itchy herbs.

When my uncle paused his assault to dig deeper into the bag for a bigger handful of poison sumac to throw all at once, Old Pat leveled the shotgun at him and took aim.

"Run!" I yelled.

The three of us high-tailed it into the shadowy forest that was between us and our getaway vehicle, and we barely made it past the tree-line before a blast rang out in the night.

"Everyone alright?" I was in shock—no one had ever shot at me before. But my first thought was to check on my friends. I could see that they were shaken, but they were both unharmed.

"We're going to need the deputy now," I said when we reached the car.

Uncle Rick was in his sixties, and he was winded and panting as he struggled to speak. "You gonna... Call him... Up here?" He bent to rest his hands on his trembling knees and catch his breath. "Then why did we take this sack of evidence?"

I was relieved to see that the bag was still bulging with a fair amount of the poison sumac leaves.

Freddie had already climbed in the car and slammed the door. "Come on, old people, let's go before we're full of holes."

I revved up the wagon and backed straight over a sapling while getting back on to the driveway. "Put on your seat belts. We're going to catch a murderer," I said.

"Isn't that why we came out here? I'm confused. Old Pat didn't sound like he had evidence of a murder to cover up out here tonight." It was Uncle Rick, fitting the clues all together and not getting the full picture. I wasn't quite there yet myself, but I had a good idea.

"No, I don't think he's guilty. Not of the two murders, anyway. But I think he just told us who is. So we're going to the hardware store to catch the true killer now."

19

Freddie dialed the deputy's number on her phone for me and put it on speaker.

"Deputy Douglas! It's Jessica Braun. If you want to catch the person who committed both recent murders, go down to Old Pat's Hardware store as quickly as you can. And bring that huge dog—Pat Junior might try to run."

I was pushing the old wagon to its limits, flooring it all the way back to town with my two cohorts in the back seat. There was no time to lose. Uncle Rick was holding on to what we had left of the proof from the shed. I knew we had to get there in the next twenty minutes if we were going to catch up to the murderer before he destroyed the rest of the evidence against him.

"What in the Sam Hill are you talking about? I'm not going down to arrest anybody at the hardware store just because you say I should."

I considered explaining to him that I'd found proof of my

suspicions, but he sounded as though he wasn't going to listen.

So I tried the one thing that I knew would get him moving.

"Okay, then meet me down there, and I will give you my confession. And all the evidence against me. Now will you grab your scary arrest-tool belt and put your boots on?" It was a risky move, but it worked.

"You admit it! I knew it was you all along. Taking after that uncle sounds like. You bet I'll be there. I'm coming to take you in for double homicide. Sheriff, come on!" He hung up the phone after calling for his canine partner.

I would need to act fast when we arrived to keep from getting handcuffed before I could show the deputy what was actually going on.

Ten minutes later, I turned off the headlights to arrive unseen, and we rolled into a parking spot in the back of the lot at Old Pat's Hardware Store. The surrounding night was empty, other than the one lone pickup truck that was idling close to the back entrance. There was no sign of the Mistletoe County Sheriff and deputy team yet. I trusted they would show up, but I didn't want to wait for them and let the evidence we needed be destroyed. We were going in.

I turned to my co-conspirators. "You both ready for this? It might not be easy."

"What do we do? You haven't explained your plan to us yet." Rick said.

I shook my head, trying to straighten out the thoughts that were almost done racing around in there, and were forming into a completed jigsaw puzzle. "There's no time right now. Just stay behind me, and make sure you bring that bag."

Uncle Rick hoisted the feed sack from Old Pat's house over one shoulder. I could see his hands were red and swollen, but I knew it would only irritate the skin. He wasn't even a bit rattled by the idea of storming into a closed store to confront a murderer. I supposed he had been through stickier situations during his life of crime.

I looked at Freddie for confirmation as I pulled the car door open to go. She was biting her lip, and I knew that meant there was something she wanted to say.

"What is it, Freddie? You can stay here where it's safe if you want—it's your choice. I don't want either of you to risk your necks with me if you don't want to." She might have been worried about what her mom would say if she came home late. I was more worried about what her mom would say to me when she found out that I had let her teenage daughter join me for a night of legally questionable adventure, but I would have to deal with that tomorrow. If I wasn't in jail for murder, that is.

"It's just that, well, I thought maybe we might need this. I found it in the grass when we were out in Mr. Peterson's backyard last night." Freddie produced a small silver cylinder with a bright red button on one end. "Deputy Douglas must have dropped it."

"Mace? Alright, Freddie. Nice one." Uncle Rick plucked it from her outstretched hand, wincing from what the toxin had done to his hands. "This ought to put that bastard in his place if he tries to get away," he said as he slipped it into the pocket of his blue jacket, that he had turned inside out to show the dark lining as better camouflage for our nighttime foray.

I wasn't crazy about bringing a weapon, but then again,

there probably wouldn't be any floor lamps at hand if I should need one for defense.

There was no more time to debate the issue. I jumped out, and they followed me as I tried to stay in the shadows along the edge of the lot.

We made our way to the employee entrance, where the truck was parked. The heavy door might be unlocked, for the killer could make a quick getaway when he finished destroying what he believed was the only proof of his crimes. Hopefully, we could get in that way and stop him in time.

I was right about the unlocked door. I pushed it open and stepped in first, like a commander leading her faithful troops into what I hoped would be a clever ambush. There was no way the killer would expect anyone to find him here tonight, so the element of surprise should be on our side.

The store was in darkness, but I saw that there was a glow coming from the office in the back of the store behind a row of riding lawn mowers. I looked back at Uncle Rick and nodded toward the light, and he nodded back. We started between the aisles in that direction, single file, with Freddie in the back and my uncle holding the pepper spray can ready.

Our footsteps echoed to the rafters in the silence, and I cringed a little at the thought that we might be discovered already. But we made it to the back wall of the store undetected. There was light coming through the window blinds beside the closed door of the office. Someone was in there, and I believed it was the person who was behind two deaths.

I was afraid to burst in and take action myself. But I was more afraid to give up now and see him get away with it, and afraid too that I might take the blame for it myself if I failed.

The deepest bark I'd ever heard sounded from the back of the store, and the responding echo bounced through every dark corner of the building.

Sheriff was on the scene, and he wanted everyone to know it.

"Mistletoe County Sheriff's Department!" The deputy's voice rang out. "Jess, I know you're in there. Give yourself up —I'm taking you in for murder!"

So much for the element of surprise—the killer definitely knew we were coming for him now.

"Quick, come on! He's going to ruin everything!" It was Freddie, speaking in a loud whisper as she pushed past my uncle and rushed toward the office door. She swung it inward and stepped to the side, letting Uncle Rick in behind her.

There, in front of the desk in the office's corner, was a large, square-shouldered man with his back to us. I saw he had a teapot and cup in front of him, and he was destroying them with a belt sander. The whine of the power tool was deafening in the small space, and I couldn't tell if he hadn't heard us coming in, or if he was just too intent on his cover-up to stop.

"Hey, Pat! Drop that sander! It's too late—we know what you did." It was a line Jessica Fletcher would've approved of, and it felt surprisingly natural to say. I realized I was starting to enjoy this amateur detective stuff.

Sheriff reached the office door first, and he was growling quietly from deep in his throat as he came in. His eyes locked onto the man holding the still-buzzing belt sander. If Pat Junior succeeded in his attempt to grind the porcelain to dust, there would be nothing left of it to test for sumac residue, making it hard to connect him to the crimes.

A moment later, Deputy Douglas came in the door. He was breathing hard from his sprint through the store to catch up with us, and his focus was on me.

I inched forward out of the deputy's reach, hoping to delay my impending arrest long enough to explain myself.

Uncle Rick stepped forward, swinging the feed sack like a club at the actual killer's hands and knocking the sander to the ground.

I was glad Freddie had dropped the pepper spray already, because the way she was hopping around and shouting, I thought she would've jabbed that red button more than once in her excitement.

Pat Junior turned to grab my uncle by the worn lapels, and that was when Sheriff made his move. Taking the whole eight feet between them in one long leap, the Great Dane threw himself at the struggling pair, knocking them both to the ground.

"Help him, Deputy Doofus! Get in there and do something!" Freddie yelled.

The confused deputy was still standing just inside the door to the room, jaw hanging open as he took in the wild scene before him. Then he seemed to make a decision and called to his dog.

"Sheriff, enough. Grab the bad guy and bring him over here."

The big canine did his job, and he dragged Pat Junior out of the scuffle by one leg, with his gigantic mouth attached to the man's boot. Pat finally gave up his hold on my uncle and relented. It had been easy for him to outwit Deputy Douglas, but there was no escaping from Sheriff.

The deputy grabbed the big man and hauled him to his feet, holding both hands behind his back, but not yet reaching for his handcuffs. He looked at me.

"Will you please tell me what's going on now, and why Sheriff is chewing on this guy? You said you were meeting me here to confess."

I knew I had a lot of explaining to do. I hoped it would be enough to make sure the deputy locked Pat Junior away instead of me and my friends.

20

"Pat Junior poisoned both my Aunt Daphne and Mr. Peterson. I can prove it to you, and then you can stop accusing me of crimes I had no part in."

I had Pat's full attention now. He was glaring up at me from where he stood, arms held behind him by Deputy Douglas. Sheriff watched him closely from where he sat beside his owner.

"I was on the wrong track for a long time. I thought it all started with Mr. Peterson, and the land deal he agreed to with Councilman Adams. With my aunt out of the way, all they had to do was convince me to sell the house in order to make a lot of money. But after Mr. Peterson was killed, too, I knew that couldn't be the case. Why would the councilman get rid of his biggest supporter? Besides, the deal had already fallen through for other reasons."

Uncle Rick asked, "Is that why you thought I was in on it —to make money? I never would have hurt my own sister, even if we didn't always see eye to eye."

I gave him an apologetic smile. "Then I found out that you knew nothing about it. I read..." I didn't actually want to mention that I had snooped in her diary—it would be an even more flagrant violation of her privacy if I allowed it to be entered into the upcoming murder trial as evidence. "... I read a lot, so I visited Ruby's Bookstore, and she told me all about her past with Daphne. I figured out that there might have been a much older motive for her murder. It was a decades-old crime of spite—the result of a youthful vendetta that ripened as a group of friends grew older, until it grew the dark fruit of murder." I was waxing poetic now, but they let me have my moment in style.

"Are you talking about Old Pat? And whatever happened to split up those friends way back when?" My uncle asked. He was following my yarn closely now as I explained how I had unraveled it.

"I can answer that." Deputy Douglas said, and I thought I would be generous and give him a moment to shine. He was the law in Pine Grove, after all. "My dad told me that Old Pat had it in for Daphne since they were just kids, and that Pat hated Mark Peterson, too. Some kind of love triangle, I guess. That Old Pat went after Mark once back then. Almost put him in the hospital."

Uncle Rick chipped in with his two cents. "And my sis and her friend from the bookstore never stopped complaining about Old Pat and his wife. Man, they were mean to Betty. They chased her out of a spaghetti dinner at the church last year—called her a pig in front of the entire congregation. She died of month later—of embarrassment, probably."

He was close to right, so I let it go. "But it wasn't Old Pat who came after my aunt and her neighbor when they wanted to tell the town the truth about the past. It was a man who acted on inherited hate and anger. Pat Junior didn't want anyone to know about father's violent history, or that the old guy was still in love with my Aunt Daphne. And he never forgot the way she treated his mother."

"But what is it he was so intent on destroying over there? I'm assuming it's some evidence?" the deputy asked.

"You're right, and I wouldn't touch that mess if I were you." I nodded toward the workbench where the old teapot Pat Junior had taken from his father's house tonight sat in pieces. "It's part of a tea service, covered with residue from the poison sumac tea he used to murder my aunt. I think he made the same brew for Mr. Peterson, but when the old man turned out to be immune to it and only had a mild reaction, Pat had to stab him to finish the job. Not everyone is allergic to poison ivy or sumac." I remembered the way Mr. Peterson had strutted straight through the poison ivy that grew in the brush between our houses without reacting, though he had to know it was there. I knew that one in five people were naturally unaffected by the active chemical in the whole family of toxic plants.

"You mean sumac tea killed Daphne?" the deputy didn't seem to notice how clueless he sounded.

I humored him and nodded. "When Pat Junior heard my aunt was coming out to talk to his father, after all these years of hard feelings between them, he knew that would be his chance. He brewed the tea with the poison sumac leaves right in it. Then when he joined his father and Aunt Daphne for tea, he made sure only she drank the special brew. Old Pat only drinks beer."

Uncle Rick set the flowered feed sack he was still holding onto the desk. "And we found the proof tonight that this jerk did it."

I explained the contents. "When we went up to Lake Sumac to look around, we went into the gardening shed and found this." I opened the cloth bag and dumped out the plant remains we'd found onto the table, careful not to let any of it contact my skin. My uncle's hands would be irritated for days from it already.

The deputy looked like he had lost track of my story a little at the last turn, so I added, "My aunt didn't go up to Lake Sumac that day to confront or threaten Old Pat, she went there to mend old fences, and to make peace with him. After Betty's death last year, she had a change of heart. It was the son who couldn't forgive the past. He fed her that poison tea during her visit. When he thought Mr. Peterson might be on to him, he poisoned him the same way."

"Then he got tired of waiting for it to work and stabbed him. What a hot-head—just like his father," Uncle Rick added.

Pat Junior snarled at us from where he was still held in the firm grip of the deputy. "That's right. I rid this town of both those old-timers. My mother never deserved the way your aunt and her friend looked at her, like they were better than her or something. I know my dad will be proud of me for taking care of them. And I would have gotten away with it too—if it hadn't been for you going up to Lake Sumac tonight like some crazed vigilante." Pat Junior glared at me, then gestured at Freddie and Uncle Rick with one elbow, unable to move his hands as they were being cuffed together by the deputy. "And those two crackpot helpers of yours— you're all just as nutty as that Daphne was."

The jab at my aunt's memory was uncalled for, and I opened my mouth to tell him so. But Freddie put a hand on my arm to calm me down and I relented. He was right after all—the entire night had been a wacky adventure, and we were a rag-tag crew. But my plan had worked, and the murderer was on his way to jail to be held accountable for his crimes. So I should take my victory and not sweat the small stuff.

"But why was he down here destroying that evidence tonight? And how did you know we would find him?" This time it was Freddie asking the questions, and I could see she was relishing our moment of triumph as budding detectives.

"The truth is, I didn't know for sure what we'd find when we arrived. When Old Pat told us that his son was at the hardware store after it was closed tonight, I thought he was possibly trying to do something here in secret. I took a chance, and it paid off." It was true. Much of my success tonight was due to a combination of guesses and luck—you can't win if you don't try.

Deputy Douglas was leading Pat Junior to the back of the waiting Mistletoe County sheriff's car while Freddie and I watched them go.

"I hope he forgets you called him a doofus." I smiled at Freddie.

We were standing outside of the hardware store, watching as the bad guy was taken away in handcuffs. Sheriff trotted proudly along in front of his deputy, looking pleased with their night's work. The dog hopped into the back seat beside him, and Pat Junior moved as far over as he could in the confined space to put some room between himself and the great four-footed lawman.

Freddie's phone was vibrating in her pocket, and when she pulled it out she said, "Holy clue in the clock. It's my mother calling."

I checked my watch and saw that it was almost eleven

thirty. I was sure Kate would be worried sick about her daughter by now.

I held my hand out, palm up. "I'll handle her for you. It's my fault you're out so late."

When I answered it, I heard a mother's chastising tone: "Freddie, here are you!? What do you think you're doing running around town past curfew? If there's still a killer on the loose..."

I cut her tirade short. "Hi there, Kate. It's Jess."

"Jess?! Oh no, has something happened to Freddie—where is she?" Kate asked.

"Freddie is with me, and she's fine. We're all fine. Deputy Douglas caught the person responsible for both murders." I wasn't sure how much to tell her about the night's events. I wanted to be honest with her about taking her mystery-crazed daughter on a possibly dangerous adventure, but I didn't want to get Freddie into trouble.

"We're downtown, at the hardware store." I answered. "I'll have her home safe and sound in a few minutes, I promise. Then I will tell you the whole story over soup at the Stonehaus tomorrow—my treat."

She agreed, and I gave Freddie back her phone. Uncle Rick caught up with us as we walked to the car.

"Is she super mad?" Freddie asked me.

"Nah, she'll get over it. She just cares about you. But I wouldn't mention taking the pepper spray." I gave her a knowing look. I didn't believe for a second that the little canister had just fallen out of Deputy Douglas's utility belt. Freddie had taken a big risk by swiping it from him, and that might be too close to a felony for Kate's comfort, as well as mine. The last thing I wanted was for Kate to decide that Freddie shouldn't help me with whatever mystery we might find ourselves in together next.

Uncle Rick had been quiet during the walk to the car, scratching at his irritated hands, and he remained silent for most of the drive. I made a mental note to find him some ointment as soon as we got home.

Back at Evergreen Circle, Freddie said goodnight and scurried off through the trees to her house, where I saw all the lights were still on inside. I hoped Kate wouldn't be too hard on her.

My uncle followed me to the door and stopped on the porch to look out over the yard.

"I really do miss her, Jess," he said to the sky that was clearing of storm clouds.

"So do I, Uncle Rick. But we can remember her by making the thrift store she dreamed of into a success." And I meant it. The thrift store was my Aunt Daphne's legacy as much as it was my future, and now that Pine Grove was safe again, I intended to stay in town and make sure the new shop would thrive.

21

TWO WEEKS LATER

"Closing time, guys. Let's lock up and get go get some dinner." The opening day of the Pine Grove Thrift Store was at an end. And nothing sounded better than warm soup in a bread bowl, a slice of chocolate cheese heaven for dessert, and a long soak in my big pink tub.

It was the first Monday in June, and two weeks had already passed since our nighttime raid at the hardware store. The three of us had been working hard, and my new business was up and running.

"We made almost fifty dollars already!" Freddie was counting out the register and grinning about our minor success. She was as proud as I was about what we'd achieved in this old garage.

Uncle Rick choked up as he turned off the lights. "My sister would be tickled pink to see this, Jess. I always knew you took after your aunt."

"Thanks," I said. "But I couldn't have done it without you two. I'm starving after that long day. Let's go."

Freddie agreed. "I need a minute to change clothes and leave a note for my mom. I'll meet you at the wagon." She bounced off to get ready for dinner.

My Uncle Rick parked himself on the front porch, swinging on Grandma's old bench. "I just want to enjoy this weather for a moment," he said. "Nothing like June in Minnesota."

He was right. Seventy degrees and full sun with a little breeze... It couldn't get any better than this.

McCoy appeared at my heels for a moment, then scampered off across the yard. I followed him and saw him start up the tree that I used to reach the attic.

I walked over to watch. The kink in his tail flexing, he made his way up to the same gutter on the second floor roof line where I'd found Uncle Rick's keys. A faint metallic tinkle drifted down to me on the wind.

I had no intention of climbing up myself this time, but I wanted to know what McCoy was doing up there. I went inside the house and up the stairs to the attic, and hurried to the attic window that looked out over the roof. Pushing the window open as far as it would go, I squeezed out onto the tiles. Careful to keep my weight balanced, I crept forward on hands and knees to where the roof ended by the tree.

"McCoy? Kitty, kitty? What in the world—"

I discovered what the sly old feline was up to. He'd been collecting his own treasures, and I had found his hiding place. I'd also just solved the mystery of the disappearing house keys.

The gutter had some clumps of old leaves and muck in it here and there, but it was full of man-made blockages as well. I saw ring after ring of keys in there—stolen not by any human criminal, but by a wily cat. McCoy had been collecting his jingling trophies all over the neighborhood by the looks of it, and he'd stashed them all away in his own personal hoard of treasures.

He appeared beside me on the roof, peering down with me at his stolen property.

"Meow?" he squeaked. He cocked his gray head to one side and looked me straight in the eye.

I was pretty sure he was asking my permission to keep them.

"Sure, buddy. Finders keepers—until somebody really needs them." I didn't know how I could explain to the neighborhood that I had keys to almost every house on the street—at least not without a good deal of awkwardness. I'd already done enough to rile up this quiet town. I ruffled McCoy's ears and scooted back to my bedroom window, leaving him to admire his hidden prizes.

Back down in the living room, I plopped myself onto my awesomely vintage but new-to-me green couch. Time for a moment's rest before dinner with my friends. This new green seat was way more comfortable than that one in Arizona had been.

My life in Pine Grove was way more comfortable, too. I'd finally found a place for myself that felt right.

The table beside me was draped with the kitten-covered feed sack and mounted by the blue fairy lamp, with the rest of the glass gems on the mantle above the small fireplace. I loved the cluttered look and homey feel of the room now that it was decorated with my favorite pieces from my aunt's collection.

Uncle Rick came in with his arms full of boxes and said,

"The mail is here."

My clothes had been delivered to the house at last, along with a handwritten note from the Pine Grove Post Office that read: *Welcome to town, Miss Braun. We're glad you didn't hurt Daphne.*

I laughed to myself as I remembered how upset the old mailman had been at my aunt's funeral. I guess he was upset enough to hold on to my packages until he was sure I wasn't a murderer. I couldn't hold it against him. My aunt still had some loyal friends in this town.

When I was dressed, we met Freddie, and drove to the Stonehaus Deli to celebrate our first day of business. Stefanie presented us all with steaming bread bowls of Chicken Tortilla soup and we took our seats in the nearly full dining room.

"Hey, do you know him?" Freddie asked me, pointing with her spoon toward where the handsome guy I'd seen here last time was standing in the doorway to the deli's kitchen—and he was staring right at us.

When I didn't answer right away, she said, "Because he looks like he knows you. Or he'd like to." She gave me a mischievous smile. "He's not bad looking for an old guy."

Tall and Dreamy must have seen us talking about him, because he started walking toward our table. I was speechless—what could he want from me?

"You want some cheesecake tonight? To go?" Of course. He was at our table in his official capacity as restaurateur. I blushed when I remembered how I embarrassed myself during my first visit to the deli.

"Of course we do. Right, Jess?" Freddie nudged me with one bony elbow.

I cleared the nerves from my throat and answered. His

dark eyes were scrutinizing me and I was starting to sweat. "Yes, I want some. Cheesecake, I mean—I want some cheesecake. To go, please."

"You got it, Jess." He smiled at me. "Two for you, and no dates." With that, he turned and went back behind the counter to box up my dessert.

"What was that about?" Freddie was giving me a wry smile. "You have talked to Joe before."

So *that's* who the handsome guy was—he was Joe Benson, who was just a neighbor kid, three grades behind me, when I'd last seen him.

That tree had certainly taken root and sprouted. "This isn't the first time I've made a fool of myself in front of him, if that's what you mean." My face and neck were burning hot from embarrassing myself again. Talking to men had never come as easily to me as sleuthing had.

"I suppose we'll be getting a new neighbor soon, now that Mr. Peterson's old place is up for sale." Uncle Rick had been busy slurping away at his soup, and was already almost finished. "I hope they won't be anyone bringing more trouble to the neighborhood."

He was right. I was ready for a peaceful summer in the quiet little town.

We had earned it. We'd rid Pine Grove of a murderer, and I had my new store to worry about. But I knew that if I found myself on the trail of another mystery, I would solve it with the help of my new friends.

My phone vibrated in my sweatshirt pocket. I didn't know the number, so I answered it cautiously. "Yes?"

"Jessie, it's Cheryl, dear. What on Earth is going on at my mother's house? I've heard you've been in all sorts of trouble, and I'm coming up there. I've booked a flight to Pine Grove."

Freddie must have read the shock on my face, because she mouthed "Hang it up," and mimed setting the phone down on the table.

But I couldn't just hang up on my own mother, even if she was a bit much sometimes. By the sounds of it, Cheryl was on her way for a visit.

"Oh, mom—er, Cheryl—you honestly don't need to do that. It's such a long flight from Hawaii, and—"

Her imperious tone cut my protest short. "Don't bother, dear. We're already on our way." That must mean she was bringing her much younger boyfriend along to Minnesota with her.

"Love you too, Cheryl, but—" She was already off the line.

"Looks like we're going to have a full house," said Uncle Rick.

That was the truth—my house, and my life, were filling up fast. But with family, not more stuff—and it was just what I needed.

Note from the author:

Hello from the north woods! I hope you had fun investigating along with Jessica Braun and her friends! I know I had a great time writing this story.

But I had even more fun writing book two in the Secondhand Sleuth Series: **An Antique Alibi**. Jessica's mother, Cheryl, was so much fun to write and I hope you will laugh a little getting to know her in the next book—while solving a murder, of course!

To connect with me and other fans, find me on Facebook at Mel Morgan Mysteries.

And don't forget to sign up at my website to get updates

and an exclusive free prequel featuring Jessica Braun: **The Salvaged Secret**.

Mel Morgan

Bonus Collector's Guide

I found my first feed sacks in my grandparents' kitchen—right in the towel drawer for everyday use.

You know those cute embroidered dish towels, often decorated with days of the week and, if you're lucky, a little kitten or rooster? Well, many of the earliest found in rural Midwestern households were originally sewn from feed sack cloth.

But that's only the plain white cloth. The fun stuff is the printed patterns in colors that often still look bright and vibrant after nearly one hundred years of storage.

Collecting authentic vintage feed sacks and farm goods made from them is a challenging but rewarding hobby. The full sacks or projects made with them don't turn up in secondhand shops every day, but when I do find a new gem for my collection, it's always worth the wait.

What is a vintage feed sack, anyway?

Vintage feed sacks are a part of farming history—and fabric history, too.

Starting in the early 1920s and continuing through the 1950s, farms received animal feed and other staples in cloth bags, or "feed sacks." The cloth that the bags were sewn from was an important commodity as well. They were made of cotton, making them soft and pliable yet durable. Women saved the material to make quilts, clothing, and even children's stuffed toys.

Before long, farm supplies were delivered in bright printed colors, and the designs they used are still appreciated today. Most feed sacks featured floral patterns, while some were decorated with whimsical animals or mid-century modern geometric patterns. Almost one hundred years later, they are still used by sewers and quilters for a variety of projects from recreating vintage quilt patterns to authentic farmhouse decor.

And it's not only crafters and quilters who collect them. Antique collectors and curators of Americana are actively seeking feed sacks and homemade projects sewn with feed sacks. That includes quilts, aprons, Christmas stockings, women's dresses, stuffed toys, and more. It's where art meets function, and it shows how early American farm families filled their lives with color and style while reusing everyday materials.

Original Feed Sack Projects

Where do you collect feed sacks, and what will it cost?

Dish towels, aprons, quilts, and dolls are all examples of items that can be hunted down at local thrift shops anywhere in the Midwest. Usually, each will only cost you a few dollars. Estate sales, particularly rural ones, are another option—though you could expect to pay at least ten or twenty dollars for each that way.

If you're looking for full sacks to create your own projects with, it can be a little trickier. Online auctions list real feed sacks, mostly from the nineteen-thirties, regularly. And they can sometimes see bids of one to two hundred dollars each. The rarest and most valuable are those featuring small prints, because they cut well for small quilt pieces, and those with unique novelty designs (like children or human figures on the rarest, or even kittens with mittens) are highly valued as well.

But if you learn to recognize the original sack fabric, you might get lucky and snag one at a small-town Midwestern thrift store in the household textiles section. Collecting them this way, each one might cost only a few dollars.

How do you identify feed sacks?

If you're looking for vintage household items made from original feed sacks, or for full sacks, there are three primary qualities to look for: texture, color, and stitching.

The texture of the vintage weave is unmistakable once you familiarize yourself with the feel. It is still pliable (and even machine washable!) and can be used like any other cotton fabric for modern projects. You can also recognize household items made from original feed sacks by knowing the color palette—lots of pale blue, medium green, bright yellow, and "cinnamon pink" (red on pink). And you can identify a full feed sack that's been opened if you can spot the stitch holes and rounded corners.

Full feed sack with opened seams

What is *reproduction* feed sack cloth?

As a quilter and fabric addict, I was introduced to reproduction feed sack prints by a local quilt show. I spotted a quilt that looked so authentically 1930s, both in pattern and fabric style, that it was hard to tell it wasn't original. Reproduction feed sack prints, which have surged in popularity among quilters over recent years, are also used for recreating farmhouse style in modern kitchens. They are a fun blend of nostalgia and novelty, and the color palette works for anything from crib quilts to home decor, but nothing beats working with the real stuff.

Reproduction Feed Sack Projects

(all photos by Mel Morgan)

Books by Mel Morgan

<u>Secondhand Sleuth Mysteries:</u>
The Vintage Vendetta
An Antique Alibi (coming soon)

Series available free on Kindle Unlimited!

Printed in Great Britain
by Amazon